WOLF HUNTED

THE LAST SHIFTER #1

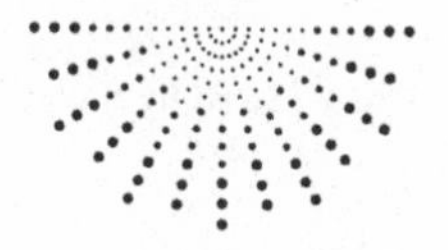

SADIE MOSS

For More Information:
www.SadieMossAuthor.com

For updates on new releases, promotions, and giveaways, sign up for my MAILING LIST.

CHAPTER ONE

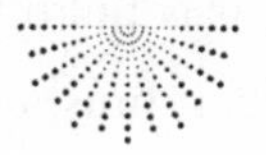

The new orderly was really cute.

At least, I assumed he was new. I'd never seen him before, and after ten years here, I was pretty sure I knew everybody at the Strand Corporation medical treatment complex. Patients came and went, and staff did too sometimes, but the turnover was slow enough that new faces always stood out.

And holy shit, *this* guy's face would stand out even in a crowd.

He had gray-blue eyes like clouds roiling with rain, framed by long, thick lashes. His features were even, dominated by a strong nose and full lips, and the tiniest hint of stubble shadowed his jaw. But the most striking thing about him was his smile. It was knock-your-sock-off brilliant, infectious, and kind. A row of even white teeth peeked out from between his lips, which quirked up a little higher on the left than the right.

And he was currently leveling that adorable, lopsided grin at me.

"Are you finished?" he asked, humor in his tone.

I blinked, realizing I was holding an empty fork halfway to my mouth. I *was*, in fact, finished with my dinner. There was nothing left on my plate, and I silently prayed that I hadn't been shoveling imaginary food into my mouth for the past five minutes while I ogled him.

Come on, Alexis. Be cool!

"Oh. Uh, yeah." I set the fork down gently beside my plate, then pushed the cafeteria-style tray across the table toward him.

"Thanks." He scooped it up, balancing the orange tray on one arm. He glanced down at it, quirking an eyebrow. "You must've enjoyed it. Is the food here any good?"

My heart thudded a little harder in my chest, and I tried to ignore it. Every time I thought I'd gotten used to my quiet, boring life in this medical complex, something came along to remind me how desperate I was for a normal life outside these walls. A life where a cute guy saying more than two words to me didn't cause my pulse to skyrocket and my mouth to dry out like sand. A life where I was more than just a patient. Where I was a normal twenty-one-year-old, going out to bars with friends on the weekends and studying for exams—all the regular things twenty-one year olds did, according to the shows I watched on the small TV in my room.

"Or... maybe not." The guy, whose name tag read *Cliff*, unleashed his devastating smile at me again.

A blush warmed my cheeks as I realized I'd zoned out. Again.

Shit. I must look like a total freak show. But a decade of living in quarantine will do that to a girl.

"Um, it's okay," I answered, forcing my mouth to form words. "I think the staff food is probably better. We have to eat exactly what Doctor Shepherd recommends. There's not a lot of variety."

He tilted his head, studying me curiously. "And you don't mind that?"

I shrugged, sitting back in my chair. My private room felt strangely small with him inside it. Orderlies stopped in every day, but they didn't usually linger to chat. I liked it, but it put me on edge too.

"It's not really a question of whether I mind or don't mind," I said. "Doctor Shepherd and his staff are keeping me alive, so I pretty much do what they tell me. If they told me to eat raw meat or tree bark, I'd probably do it."

The orderly ran his free hand through his dark blond hair, tousling the short spikes. He dipped his head in a nod, a serious expression crossing his face. "Huh. Makes sense, I guess. Well, I hope they at least have the decency to let you have dessert once in a while."

I smiled broadly. "Don't worry, they do. Life isn't worth living without dessert."

He chuckled. The sound poured over me like warm honey, sparking a swarm of butterflies in my stomach. Not that I had a whole lot of experience with this sort of thing, but I was beginning to think he might be flirting with me.

That thought made me so nervous my throat threatened to close up, so I shoved it away. Besides, why would a guy like him flirt with a girl like me? It wasn't like I was hideous or anything. The brown hair that fell to my mid-back was a pretty chocolate color, and although I wasn't allowed to wear makeup—in case any of the ingredients caused a negative reaction—my mom assured me I didn't need it. She said my golden eyes and high cheekbones did all the work for me, and makeup would only get in the way of my natural beauty.

Thanks, mom.

Still, I couldn't imagine this guy would have any problem finding a date out in the real world—where he could actually, you know, take the girl *out*. The closest thing to a date in this place would be a trip to the cafeteria or the exercise yard, under the watchful eyes of half a dozen doctors and lab techs.

Not the most romantic activity in the world.

Which was why dating was off the table for me until the day when—or *if*—I finally got out of here. Doctor Shepherd was always careful to remind me and my mom that my treatment had no end date set in stone. He was optimistic that one day they'd cure me, but he refused to make any promises.

I appreciated that. I didn't want him offering platitudes or false hope. But even though he reminded me often that I might not ever be able to survive outside this place, I couldn't believe that. I *knew* someday I'd walk out of here completely healed. I had to.

"Well... I'll get out of your hair. Didn't mean to distract you; you look like you've got a lot on your mind."

The orderly flashed me another smile and backed away from the small table in my room, turning toward the door.

Damn it! I'd zoned out again. What on earth was wrong with me? It wasn't like I'd never encountered another human being down here. My mom visited me weekly, and I saw staff and other patients often. So why was I so completely brain-fried around this particular guy?

Maybe it had something to do with the fact that most of the Strand staff were at least twice my age, and the patients tended to keep to themselves. Some of them were much sicker than me, which made socializing hard.

"No, it's fine!" I blurted, too emphatically. "I like the company. You can... stop by anytime."

The grin he tossed back over his shoulder practically made me melt.

When he closed the door behind him, I hauled myself off my chair and face-planted on the twin bed in the corner. Rolling over onto my back, I draped an arm over my face, shoving my long hair out of the way.

"Seriously, Alexis. What is wrong with you?" I muttered.

My only consolation was that if he was a new staff

member, he would most definitely be back.

Not because of my lame invitation, but because it was his job.

Whatever. I'd take it. And next time he came, I wouldn't be such a goofy mess. Maybe I could actually string a few words together and sound semi-coherent. I'd spent enough hours in this room reading and re-reading the books my mom brought me that I should be able to hold my own in intelligent conversation.

Just so long as he doesn't smile.

Rolling my eyes, I groped around on the nightstand until I found my current novel, *Pride and Prejudice.* I'd read it before, but since I could only fit a limited number of books on the bookshelf in my small room at one time, I'd given it to my mom a while ago in exchange for something new. She'd brought it back on her last visit, and I was halfway through Darcy and Elizabeth's love story. Right around the part where Darcy was acting like a huge dick, actually, which inexplicably made me like him even more. Maybe it was because I knew the twist was coming, where his softer side would be revealed.

Or maybe I just found something attractive about assholes.

That orderly, Cliff, didn't seem like an asshole though.

My stomach warmed again at the thought of him. Definitely not an asshole. He'd radiated warmth and kindness, and despite my awkwardness and nerves, his presence had made me feel at ease.

I read for a while, getting lost between the pages, but my mind kept wandering back to a pair of startling gray-blue eyes. Finally, I put the book back down, glancing over at the clock on the wall. *8:45*. In fifteen minutes, the medical complex would begin shutting down for the night. We didn't have an official curfew here, but considering all the doors locked at 9 p.m., the end result was pretty much the same.

But if I hurried, I could still make it to the cafeteria and swipe a snack for later.

Sliding the bookmark into place, I set *Pride and Prejudice* back on the nightstand. Then I hopped up from the bed and pulled a pair of simple black flats from the closet. I no longer had to wear hospital gowns all the time like I had the first few years I was here, but my wardrobe choices had never moved far beyond yoga pants and simple t-shirts. Who was there to impress down here?

When I stepped out of my room, the hallway was empty. I wasn't surprised. This place was quiet as the grave at night. I didn't consider myself a particularly adventurous person, but I was a downright wild child compared to some of the other patients who lived here. We were each allowed to decorate our private suites with small alterations, but I was the only person who had any posters or art on my walls.

Those things and my books were my ode to the outside world, a reminder to myself that there were bigger things beyond these walls.

The Strand Corporation medical complex was a windowless structure, built underground to make it easier for them to shield us from airborne pathogens. There were levels below us that housed labs, operating rooms, hospitals beds, and medical equipment, but I rarely left the main floor. Everything I needed for day-to-day life was on this level, so there was little reason to.

As I walked down the brightly lit, gray tiled hallway, I sent up a silent prayer of gratitude for the millionth time. I had no idea how much it cost to house me in this state-of-the-art treatment facility, but I knew it was way more than my mom earned on her teacher's salary. If the Strand Corporation hadn't offered to treat me at no expense, I definitely wouldn't be here now.

I likely wouldn't be alive either.

Most of my childhood memories were fuzzy, but I vividly remembered the sight of lights flashing overhead as I was wheeled down hallways into what seemed like an endless stream of emergency rooms. After dozens of baffled doctors and near-death experiences, I'd finally been diagnosed with an incredibly rare autoimmune disease called Speyer's Syndrome.

The diagnosis would've been a curse, except for the fact that my illness was interesting and strange enough to garner the attention of the Strand Corporation, one of the largest biomedical research firms in the country. They'd approached my mom with an offer—their doctors would undertake my treatment for free as a means of studying my disease. They never promised to cure me, but it was still a no-brainer for my mom. It was a chance at hope when we'd had none left.

And so far, the treatment seemed to be working. They hadn't fixed me permanently, but with the regimen of meds, exercise, and limited contact with outside pathogens, I felt fine most days and was able to live a normal life.

Or as normal as possible while locked away from human society, anyway.

I knocked on the wall as I passed, hoping there was wood somewhere under the plaster. I'd developed a few superstitious habits over the years, and I was a huge believer in staying on luck's good side. She'd helped me out a lot so far; I saw no reason to piss her off.

Picking up the pace, I cut through the large, open room that formed the hub of the entire complex, turning down another hallway toward the cafeteria. If I didn't hurry, I'd miss my chance. I had a key card to my own room, but I'd be locked out of every other room in the place at nine o'clock sharp.

Half the lights in the cafeteria were already off. The kitchen was closed down, but an array of snacks and small meals—all Doctor Shepherd-approved—were on display in an open refrigeration unit.

I grabbed an apple and a banana. A little boring, but they'd have to do. All that talk of dessert with the cute orderly had made me crave something sweet.

As I turned back toward the entryway, the grate that closed off the cafeteria at night began to drop from the ceiling with a grinding, rattling sound. I'd cut the timing too close.

"Fuck!" I muttered under my breath.

Clutching my fruit, I raced toward the wide doorway, dropping to the floor at the last second and rolling under the descending metal partition. I felt it brush my shoulder before I emerged on the other side, feeling so much like Indiana Jones I almost reached back for my hat.

I let out a little whoop, then snapped my mouth shut when the sound echoed too loudly in the quiet, empty space. I raised my prizes triumphantly, taking a bite of the apple as I strode back down the hall. I felt strangely buzzed, excitement thrumming through my veins and making my heart beat faster.

Maybe tonight I'd stay up late and finish reading *Pride and Prejudice.* Doctor Shepherd was always hounding me about getting enough rest, but I wasn't tired at all, and I didn't have anything pressing to do tomorrow. Maybe I'd live a little and—

A wave of dizziness hit me out of nowhere. I staggered to a halt, sweat breaking out on my skin. Sharp pain tore through me, lighting up my nerve endings like a hot poker. My muscles contracted, and I stumbled, falling to my knees and pitching sideways.

The hand holding the banana squeezed too tightly, crushing the yellow skin until white fruit oozed out from the cracks like pus.

As my body jerked and twisted in a seizure, I watched the apple roll away from me across the smooth marble floor.

No. Not like this. Please, not like this.

CHAPTER TWO

My limbs jerked and spasmed, no longer under my control.

The warm yellow lights set along the hallway wall bounced in my vision as my eyes began to slide out of focus. I could feel myself being pulled under, my body shutting down. Pain lanced through me in sharp jolts, gone one second and back with agonizing ferocity the next, as if an invisible knife were stabbing me.

No. This can't be happening! I've been doing so well.

The fuzzy thoughts ricocheted through my brain, trying to find a place to land. I couldn't focus on anything but the lights flashing in my periphery. I hadn't had an attack this bad since right after I came to live here, and this was worse than anything I remembered. It felt different. More terrifying.

As if some part of me was trying to rip its way out—like my body was tearing itself into pieces.

An alarm sounded, and footsteps pounded down the hall.

"Alexis?" a male voice yelled in the distance, but the sound reached my ears as a muffled whisper.

Doctor Shepherd. Help.

"Damn it! She's seizing!"

"When did this happen?" Doctor Shepherd demanded. "What went wrong?"

"I don't know, sir. She was fine, then she just went down."

"Shit. Help me! Hold her still."

Fingers lifted my eyelids, and a new bright light assaulted my senses. I was vaguely aware of muffled grunts and groans coming from my mouth, and of strong hands latching onto my arms and legs.

"We need to get her downstairs." The light shining in my eyes cut off, and Doctor Shepherd's pale face swam in front of me. His blue eyes were anxious, and his eyebrows pinched together. "Put her on the gurney. Now!"

The hands holding my limbs lifted me, and I was placed on a new, higher surface. My body kept thrashing and jerking, and my brain felt like it was rattling in my skull. I tried to speak—to apologize for letting them all down, to beg for help, to scream my frustration to the heavens—but I could barely form thoughts, let alone words.

Tight leather straps pressed across my chest, midsection, and legs, restraining the movement of my body. Then the wheels of the gurney began to roll, and I was carted swiftly down the hall, surrounded by doctors on all sides. Tears spilled from my eyes, rolling down the sides of my face, as I stared up at the ceiling tiles gliding by overhead. The sight was so horribly familiar it sent dread spiraling through me.

There was a soft *ding*, and a moment later, I was wheeled into a large elevator. Tense silence filled the space, broken only by the rustling sound of my body jerking and my hoarse grunts.

"Is it happening?"

The soft voice was female, but I couldn't place who it belonged to. Maybe Claudia, one of the older female nurses on staff.

"Shh." Another voice shushed her.

Doctor Shepherd's face hovered over me again, his hands resting on my shoulders. "Alexis. Can you hear me? You're going to be all right. We've got you."

Even as he spoke, I could feel myself fading. I clung to consciousness like a life raft, afraid if I let myself slip under, I'd never come back. I'd seen other patients collapse and be wheeled away, and they almost never returned.

No. I'm not ready to die.

I fought against the muscle spasms rocking my body and tightened my hands into fists, willing luck to come through for me one more time. To let me be the medical miracle who beat the odds. To give me one more chance.

The elevator slid to a stop, and I was rushed down another long hallway, this one all white. I knew that because I'd been down here a few times before, although right now everything around me looked gray as my vision began narrowing to a pinprick.

"Damn it! We're losing her! Hurry!"

Doctor Shepherd's panicked voice bounced off the walls.

My eyes rolled back in my head, blackness finally overtaking me.

I drifted, lost in a sea of darkness where my body didn't hurt. There was nothing bad here, but there was nothing good either. It was just... nothing.

Flashes of light and sound occasionally burst into my consciousness as if someone had turned on a television with the volume all the way up.

"Intubating now!"

A tube was forced down my throat, making me cough and gag.

Then darkness again.

Now I clung to the darkness, the peaceful emptiness, not wanting to return to that room full of chaos and pain.

But I was pulled back by a sharp tearing sound. My eyes flew open as my body sprang upright, and I saw the leather straps that had held me down dangling in pieces beside me. My head whipped around, a feral scream tearing from my mouth.

"Alexis! No!" Doctor Shepherd's harsh cry drew my attention, and I turned toward him. He dove toward me, a needle in his hand. Before I could move, the needle pierced my skin, and with a pneumatic hiss, the contents emptied inside me.

I fell back, and the world dissolved around me.

~

"Jesus, that was close."

"I know. We should've been monitoring her more carefully."

"With all due respect, Doctor Shepherd, I don't see how we could've monitored her more closely. We got to her as quick as we could."

"And it almost wasn't quick enough. I want her to be checked twice as often going forward. We're entering a critical time."

Doctor Shepherd's voice was quiet and tired-sounding. Worry weighed down his words. As hazy memories of my episode began to filter into my mind, I felt my heart swell to think that he cared that much. Doctor Shepherd had been the head of the team of doctors assisting me since the first day I arrived here, and even though I was partly just a research project, I'd always felt like he was personally invested in my care beyond that.

I was more than just a body on a gurney to him. I was a person.

My eyelids fluttered, and a small noise escaped me. The hushed conversation around me stopped, and when I opened my eyes, Doctor Shepherd stood over me once again.

"Hey there, Alexis." He smiled gently, but it didn't quite reach his eyes. "You gave us all quite a scare."

"Sorry." The word felt like a cheese grater on my throat, and I swallowed. My mouth was bone dry.

The middle-aged doctor shook his head. He had bright blue eyes that were often puffy and always a little bloodshot, and today the bags under them were especially pronounced. "Hey, now. You don't have anything to be sorry for. It wasn't your fault. I'm just glad you're still with us."

I tried to chuckle, but it hurt too much. "Me too."

"I'm going to give you something for the pain, okay? It'll knock you out a bit and give you a chance to rest some more. We've got your levels back to where they should be, but your body still needs some time to recover."

Opting not to speak, I dipped my chin in a small nod.

Doctor Shepherd hooked up a new bag to my IV drip, and a moment later, the cocktail of drugs stole me away.

When I woke again, it was to a quiet room filled only with the steady beep of a heart rate monitor and the thrum of a computer.

I blinked slowly. My whole body felt stiff and tired. I was propped up in a hospital bed, covered in a thin sheet and dressed in a medical gown.

But the pain was gone.

I licked my cracked lips and felt around me for the call button. A moment later, Claudia poked her head into the room.

"Ah! Look who's awake!" The elderly nurse beamed at me as if I'd done something much more impressive than simply lift my eyelids. She bustled into the room, her short, plump frame straining inside her one-size-too-small scrubs. "Do you need something, sweetheart?"

"Water," I said, my voice weak. My throat didn't hurt anymore though.

"I'll do you one better. Here." She lifted a plastic cup with a closed lid and straw off the counter. It contained a clear pinkish liquid. "This will help with your electrolyte balance too. Drink up. I'll go get Doctor Shepherd."

The round-faced woman handed me the cup and turned away.

"Claudia?" I called. She stopped, glancing over her shoulder at me. "What happened? Why did I collapse? I've been doing so well."

She sighed, squinting at me. "You had a little setback, dear. You really have been doing amazingly well, and you shouldn't let this discourage you. Doctor Shepherd adjusted your meds, and it seems to be working very well."

I nodded, although I knew it couldn't be nearly as simple as she made it sound. I'd almost died. I had *felt* it.

"Okay. Thanks." She turned to leave, but my voice stopped her again. "Hey, Claudia? My memory is kinda fuzzy, but when we were in the elevator, I think you asked if 'it' was happening. What did you mean? What was happening?"

For a second, her face went entirely blank. She stared at

me, blinking quickly, then shook her head and gave a rueful laugh.

"Oh, dear. Nothing, sweetie. I didn't mean anything. I was just worried about you. I wouldn't have said anything if I thought you could hear me; the last thing I want to do is scare you." She crossed back over to the bed, cupping my cheek in her warm, soft hand. "We've all gotten quite attached to you."

A lump rose in my throat, and I dipped my head, breaking away from her touch. "Thanks, Claudia."

"Of course, dear." She stepped back, straightening her blue scrubs. "I really don't want you to worry. I know that was scary, but it was just a minor setback. Doctor Shepherd says everything is back on track now. I'll go get him so you can ask him yourself."

She bustled out the door, leaving me alone in the room with the quiet beeping. I cleared my throat, blinking against the tears that stung my eyes as I brought the straw to my lips. The liquid was sweet and tasted vaguely like strawberries.

I was so grateful for everything Doctor Shepherd and his staff had done for me. And I was attached to *them* too. They'd become like a surrogate family to me, people I saw even more often than my own mother. But unease settled in my belly as I recalled the look on Claudia's face.

She'd seemed almost... frightened.

Had I been closer to death than they were letting on? I felt fine now, but how much could I trust that? Were they lying about my recovery progress? Maybe they just didn't want to admit defeat.

Before my thoughts could spiral any further, the door cracked open again, and Doctor Shepherd poked his head in. The smile on his face soothed my nerves instantly. He strode in, glancing down at my chart before meeting my gaze.

"Good news, super trooper." He beamed down at me. "We've got you back on track. You'll be able to go back to your own suite soon."

CHAPTER THREE

Doctor Shepherd insisted on having me brought up to the main level in a wheelchair, which was embarrassing and disheartening. But I hadn't been kidding when I told that cute orderly, Cliff, I'd do whatever the doctor told me to. He had my life in his hands, and my survival depended on following his orders exactly.

That, and maybe a little bit of luck.

I was a bedraggled mess when I finally got to my room. I'd been downstairs in the ICU for over a week so they could monitor me as I recovered from my episode—which I would've considered overkill if the whole incident hadn't scared me so badly. But now I felt disgusting from several days without a shower, as if a gross film coated my entire body.

Marianne, a nurse with squinty eyes and a loud laugh,

wheeled me inside, keeping up a running stream of one-sided conversation the entire time.

Cliff looked up in surprise from where he was changing the sheets on my bed. "Oh, hey!" He peered at me more closely. "You okay?"

My cheeks felt like they were on fire, and I looked down, letting my tangled brown hair shield my face. So much for making a good impression the next time I saw him. "Yeah, I'm fine. I just need a shower."

I stood up, as anxious to wash off the 'intensive care patient ick' as I was to get out of Cliff's sight. But Doctor Shepherd had obviously had a good reason for ordering the wheelchair—my legs buckled as soon as I put all my weight on them, and I stumbled.

Cliff darted toward me, his gray-blue eyes flashing with concern, and caught me under the arms before I went down. The muscles of his large biceps contracted against the sleeves of his scrubs, although it didn't look like it took him any effort to hold me up.

I blinked up at him stupidly, drowning in the soft blue of his eyes. My arms had gone around his neck instinctively, and his skin was warm and smooth under my fingertips.

He was taller than I'd realized. I had to tilt my head back quite a bit to meet his gaze. A little line appeared between his brows as he frowned down at me, then he glanced over my shoulder at Marianne and set me back gently in the wheelchair.

He cleared his throat. "Well, I'll leave you to it.

Marianne, can you finish the bed?"

"Of course."

Keeping his head down, Cliff slipped past us and out the door. A trickle of embarrassment slid down my spine. Damn it. He'd seemed really anxious to get out of here. Maybe I really did stink. I tried to surreptitiously sniff my armpits as Marianne pushed me into the bathroom. I couldn't smell anything, but that probably didn't mean much. Wasn't it true you couldn't smell your own B.O.?

Marianne helped me to the seat in the shower then left the door cracked while she went to make up the bed. Her one-sided conversation picked up again, and I wondered if she knew or cared that I could barely hear her over the sound of the water.

Probably not.

When I finally felt clean, I used a rail on the side of the shower to help pull me to my feet. My legs held this time, although I felt a little lightheaded and wobbly. Doctor Shepherd seemed to think I was okay, so this was probably just regular muscle weakness from being in bed for a week. I walked slowly out of the shower and was halfway dressed by the time Marianne poked her head back in.

"Look at you!" She clapped her hands, smiling proudly at me. "Back on your feet already. You'll be back to usual in no time! Doctor Shepherd has you booked for training sessions every day this week starting tomorrow. He doesn't want you to lose too much ground because of this."

I groaned. "Every *day*?"

She chuckled understandingly. “Afraid so. I’m sure you’ll have fun. At least it passes the time, right?”

“I guess so. I’m pretty sure Erin’s trying to kill me though.”

Her thick lips pursed. “Now, that’s the last thing she’s trying to do, and you know it.”

“Yeah, yeah, I know,” I sighed. “It’s all for my own good.”

“Exactly.”

Marianne helped me out of the bathroom and to my bed, although I barely needed her steadying hand anymore. My legs were recovering fast. She left a few minutes later, reminding me to use the call button if I needed anything.

I spent the rest of the day lounging in my room, reading and recovering. I’d become an expert in passing time over the years, but now I found myself oddly restless—so much so that by the next day, I was actually looking forward to my session with Erin.

In one spoke of the wheel shape that made up the Strand complex, we had a huge training yard. It was outfitted with overhead lights that replicated sunlight and had just about every piece of equipment I could imagine. A large open space in the middle was covered by a soft green material probably meant to simulate grass. A track ran around the entire oval-shaped space.

Patients were allowed into the yard even when we didn’t have training sessions, so I spent a lot of time here. It was the closest we got to having access to the outdoors, even though it was a pretty poor imitation.

Doctor Shepherd was a stickler for holistic treatment. In addition to the cocktail of meds we were given daily, our diet and exercise were closely monitored.

There were some patients who were too sick to do much physical activity, but I wasn't one of those unlucky ones—or *lucky* ones, as I thought to myself some days. Erin, my trainer, always pushed me hard, leaving me sweaty and exhausted by the end of our sessions. But as much as I complained about them, I relished them too. They were a reminder that I wasn't dead yet. That my body was still fighting.

"Glad to see you back on your feet."

Erin smiled at me as I approached. She was short and broad, all stocky muscle and spiky dark hair. I was in pretty good shape, thanks to my work with her, but I'd never match her level of muscle tone.

"Good to be back on my feet." I smiled wanly, pushing away the memory of stumbling out of my wheelchair. Nothing scared me as much as feeling weak. It made me feel like death was just waiting to pick me off, like a vulture circling a dying animal.

Erin noticed the pinched expression on my face and clapped me heavily on the arm. "Don't worry. We'll get you back in tip-top shape in no time. You're one of my best patients. I won't let you give up."

I nodded determinedly, gathering up my long brown hair into a tight ponytail. Over the next hour and a half, she put me through dozens of drills, mostly bodyweight exercises that challenged my strength and agility. I *had* lost some ground after my time in the ICU, but as my heart rate picked up and my breath quickened, I could feel my body falling into the groove again.

The next day's session was a little easier, and the day after that too.

By the end of the week, I could almost forget my brush with death had ever happened.

At least, until my mother came to visit.

"Mom, I'm okay! Really."

The words were almost unintelligible since I spoke them into her armpit. She was a good eight inches taller than me. My dad had died when I was little, but I'd definitely gotten my diminutive 5'3" height from him.

But my mom either didn't hear or didn't believe me, because her death grip on me only tightened further.

"I was so worried about you, baby girl."

I sighed, giving up my struggle and wrapping my arms around her. She only called me "baby girl" when she was really worried. Sometimes I felt like she forgot I'd been growing up this whole time—as if I'd been put into some kind of stasis when I came to live at the Strand complex ten years ago.

Hell, sometimes it felt that way to me too. I was twenty-one, but I had no clue how to be a normal twenty-one-year-old.

She rocked me back and forth before finally stepping back to hold me at arm's length. Her eyes scanned my face, searching for any hint of distress. "Are you all right? Doctor Shepherd said your bloodwork looks good, but how do you *feel*?"

I looked away, avoiding her gaze. "I feel... fine."

Her eyes narrowed. "You paused."

Oops. The woman was an expert in seeing through my bullshit.

I walked over to the small couch set against the back wall and plopped onto it. My mom followed, watching me carefully through her thick glasses. Leaning against one end, I drew my legs up to my chest and turned to look at her.

"I do feel fine, Mom. That's the problem. I went from fine, to almost dead, to fine again in the space of two weeks. It makes me..." I swallowed, gritting my teeth against the tears that wanted to come. "It makes me not trust 'fine.' It makes me think this will never be over."

Understanding filled her expression. Her caramel brown eyes, so similar to my own, softened. "It will be, Alexis. One day, you'll be cured. Doctor Shepherd and his staff are working so hard. You've come so far. You just have to keep believing."

I drew in a breath, trying to find the same faith and confidence she had. I'd held onto it for so long, but this last episode had shaken me to the core. For the first time in years, I found myself contemplating what would happen if I was never cured. Could I live my whole life like this? Confined to this medical complex forever—never stepping foot in the outside world? Never experiencing something as simple and basic as going on one stupid date?

Was that really a life worth living?

And even more terrifying, what would happen if the powers that be at the Strand Corporation came to the same conclusion? If my illness was incurable, was I still worth studying? Or would they kick me out of here eventually, leaving me to fend for myself?

My mom seemed to read all the fears and doubts passing through my mind as if I'd spoken them out loud. She brushed a lock of hair back from my face, tucking it behind my ear. "Don't give up, Alexis. I know it's so hard. But nothing has changed. You're still the amazing fighter you always were. Just keep doing what Doctor Shepherd and the others tell you, and you'll beat this."

I leaned into her touch, closing my eyes for a moment. I didn't want her to see the doubt that still reflected in them.

When I met her gaze again, I forced a smile to my lips. "Thanks, Mom. But enough about me and boring medical stuff. How are you? How are classes?"

She smiled, letting me redirect the conversation. "I'm good. Classes are exhausting. And summer is almost here."

I chuckled. With her glasses and gray-streaked brown hair cut in a classic bob, my mom looked like the quintessential middle school teacher—so it was hardly surprising she'd ended up in that job. Sort of like how guys named Chad were destined to grow up to be douchebags. She seemed to love it, but it was around this time of year that she got as antsy for the summer break as her students.

"What are you going to do over the summer?"

She relaxed back into the couch cushions, considering. "Read some books I've been meaning to pick up. Do a little gardening. And visit you a lot more."

"That would be nice."

Not just for me, but for her too. I worried about her, even though it was probably silly. But with my dad gone and her only child stuck in a medical complex three hours from her home in Austin, I hoped she wasn't too lonely. Work kept her busy, but I knew firsthand that filling up your days didn't always stave off loneliness and heartache.

"Yes, I think so." The little lines around her mouth deepened as she smiled. Then she sat up straighter, plucking her purse off the couch beside her. "Oh, I almost forgot. I brought you more contraband!"

She pulled several fat books out of her bag, and my face lit up with genuine excitement for the first time since she'd arrived. My mom always knew the perfect thing to get me out of a funk.

We spent several more hours talking and laughing, and by the time she left, I felt a lot better.

But as the door closed behind her, a dark cloud seemed to roll into the room. I stared around at the small space, and despite the years I'd spent here, it felt foreign and sterile.

How much longer could I live like this?

And what other choice did I have?

CHAPTER FOUR

"How have you been feeling, Alexis?"

I clenched my jaw, trying not to let my irritation show. The number of times I'd been asked that over the course of my lifetime was staggering. I knew the question came from a good place, but I'd have given anything to never hear those words again.

"Fine."

"That's good," Doctor Shepherd said approvingly. His face hovered inches from mine as he shone a small light into my eyes. I was never sure where to look during these exams, although I probably should've figured it out by now. It felt awkward to look away, but equally awkward to stare straight into his eyes. So my gaze darted around the room like a butterfly, flitting from place to place without really landing on anything.

"Look up," he directed. I obeyed. "Good. And down."

I followed his directive, and he nodded with satisfaction before moving around to peer into each ear.

"Erin tells me your sessions with her have been going well. And how are your new meds treating you?"

"Fine." I tensed slightly as he adjusted the back of my hospital gown to place the end of the stethoscope between my shoulder blades. His fingers were always cold. "I've been a little lethargic, especially at night, but not too bad."

"That's fine." His voice was as calm and soothing as ever. "That's an expected side effect. If it gets to be too much, we can adjust your dose. Breathe in."

My ribs expanded as I pulled in a deep lungful of air. Then I released it slowly. Despite the paper covering the exam table, the chill of the metal seeped into my legs. The gown was tied at the back of my neck, but all I had on beneath it was a pair of underwear, and as Doctor Shepherd's chilly fingers moved the stethoscope to a new spot on my back, goose bumps raised the hair on my arms.

He listened to me take a few more long breaths before pulling the stethoscope out of his ears and draping it around his neck. He retied the gown at my mid-back, then grabbed my chart and sat on his rolling stool, using his feet to steer it a little closer to the exam table where I perched.

"Well, everything looks good, kiddo. I think we're back on track. Do you have any questions for me?"

The word "no" was on the tip of my tongue, but when I opened my mouth, what actually came out was, "Do you think I'm going to die in here?"

Doctor Shepherd stopped writing on my chart.

He looked up at me slowly, little crow's feet pinching the corners of his eyes as he squinted. "Why do you say that, Alexis?"

I swallowed, wishing like hell I could take back what I'd just blurted. This was supposed to be a medical exam, not a counseling session. But while he'd promised me I was doing all right physically, I was anything *but* okay mentally and emotionally. I felt like I'd been waiting for the other shoe to drop my entire life, and now it was hanging over me. I had no idea why I'd suddenly lost my faith in the healing process, why I'd suddenly become so impatient for a resolution. I wanted to get my equilibrium back, but I had no clue where to find it.

"I... I don't know. I guess lately I've just started to wonder if it's ever going to happen. If I'll ever be cured. I mean, what if I'm not? Will you guys really take care of me forever?"

Doctor Shepherd regarded me seriously, resting his elbows on his knees and lacing his fingers together. "I can't say anything with one hundred percent certainty, you know that. I won't give you false promises. But I will tell you this, Alexis. Everyone in this building is invested in you. You are important to us. Beyond the science. Beyond the medicine. *You* are important to us."

A warm feeling bloomed in my chest, and even though it was sort of awkward having this conversation with my doctor, his words helped a lot.

"Thanks, Doc." I scratched my ear, blushing slightly. "I

guess it's just good to know you guys see me as more than my disease."

"You're much more than that, Alexis." He smiled, rubbing the small tattoo on the inside of his wrist with the thumb of his opposite hand. It wasn't a cross, but I was pretty sure it was some kind of religious symbol. "There are things in this world even science can't explain yet. Faith is important. Have you visited the chapel recently?" He held up his hands, chuckling softly. "I'm not going to tell you who to pray to, but I will tell you it's important that you believe in something. Without hope, without *faith*, what is any of this for?"

The sentiment was so similar to what I often told myself that I glanced up to meet his gaze, surprised. I hadn't visited the chapel in weeks—it was set in another spoke that extended out from the main hub, one I didn't venture down often. But when I used to go more regularly, I sometimes saw Doctor Shepherd there.

"How do you find the balance?" I asked, aware this conversation was veering into strange territory, but unable to tamp down my curiosity. "Between faith and science?"

Doctor Shepherd's smile widened, and his eyes gleamed with excitement. "I don't need to, kiddo. At some point, the two intersect. And that's where miracles happen."

He looked almost like a kid talking about his favorite game or a new toy. His enthusiasm was contagious, and I found a little of my old confidence returning.

That's where miracles happen.

I could be a miracle. I could beat the odds.

Running a hand down my arm to smooth the goose bumps that still lingered there, I grinned back at him. "I like that. Thanks, Doctor Shepherd."

"No problem, Alexis." He wheeled back toward the small desk in the corner, peering at my chart. "Now, I've got you—"

A sound in the distance interrupted him, and he broke off abruptly, lifting his head.

The sound came again.

A rapid *pop-pop-pop,* as if someone were setting off firecrackers down the hall.

"What's that?"

Even as I asked, a cold feeling flooded me, and my heart stuttered in my chest.

Before he could answer, shouts and screams echoed from down the hallway, followed by the sound of feet pounding against the tiled floor. An alarm blared through the complex, so loud and shrill it made me jump. I'd never heard a siren like this, not even when one of the patients coded like I had.

Doctor Shepherd froze. His eyes went wide, and he half stood from his stool, a shocked expression on his face.

I threw my hands over my ears, trying to block out the screeching siren as I yelled over its noise. "What's happening? What is it?"

He didn't answer.

My heart was galloping in my chest now, confusion and fear twisting my insides. Whatever this was, it wasn't normal. It wasn't even on the far edge of normal.

It was wrong, and very, very bad.

The handle of the only door into the room rattled. I yelped, turning toward it. The door didn't open, and the handle shook harder. *Locked.* Had it always been locked? Or was it some kind of automatic shutdown that went along with the sirens?

It didn't matter in a second though, because two more loud pops sounded, and the lock blew away in a shower of splinters. The door flew open as someone kicked it from the other side, and Doctor Shepherd finally leapt into action. He threw himself toward me, the force of his movement sending the rolling stool careening into the wall behind him. His hand latched around my upper arm, dragging me off the exam table.

Another pop of gunfire filled the room, louder and closer this time, and I screamed. Doctor Shepherd grunted in pain, releasing his grip on me. Blood sprayed from a wound on his arm as he staggered backward, going down near the medical supply cabinet along one wall.

I stood in the middle of the room, numb with shock, as the man with the gun strode inside, his steps smooth and controlled as a stalking cat. He was striking, with short, wavy brown hair and a slightly crooked nose that looked like it'd been broken at least once. He must've been close to my age, but the hard expression on his face made him look older.

He swept the gun around the room before training it on Doctor Shepherd again.

"Where's Sariah?" he growled.

"Sariah?" Doctor Shepherd inched backward toward the wall, gripping his wounded arm with one hand. Blood welled between his fingers. "I... I don't know who that is."

"Goddamnit." The man sneered in disgust. "Of course you don't. Why learn their names, right?"

More shouts came from outside. Raised, angry voices. More feet running. I stood paralyzed, my gaze darting back and forth between the intruder and Doctor Shepherd.

"I don't know what you're talking about," Doctor Shepherd gasped. He'd wedged himself into a nook where the cabinet met the wall, and he grimaced in pain as blood continued to seep from his right arm, staining the sleeve of his white lab coat.

"Sariah!" the man repeated, both hands steadying his weapon. "Eighteen years old. Black hair. She was at the compound outside San Diego before they shut it down. Is she here?"

Something shifted in Doctor Shepherd's face. The fear that had twisted his features faded, replaced by an almost condescending glare. "No. She's not here."

The new man swore softly under his breath. His gaze flicked to me, and for the first time since he'd entered, he seemed to truly take me in. I was only wearing a hospital gown, and under the scrutiny of his amber eyes, I felt completely naked, as if he could see right through to my soul.

His attention lingered on me for a second too long... and in that second, Doctor Shepherd moved.

Letting go of his injured arm, the doctor slid his left hand behind the medical supply cabinet. When he pulled it out, a gun was clutched in his grip.

The intruder's head whipped back toward him, his hand tightening on his own weapon.

Two shots pierced the air.

CHAPTER FIVE

I covered my ears as the gunshots rang out, screaming into the void of noise and chaos.

A hole appeared in the wall inches from Doctor Shepherd's head, and the shot he'd fired toward the brown-haired intruder went wide.

The man dove to the side as Doctor Shepherd aimed again. A third shot echoed in the sterile room as the man slammed into me, bringing me to the floor with a heavy thud. We landed behind the large metal exam table, its hefty bulk separating us from Doctor Shepherd.

For a split second, I was acutely aware of the muscled body pressed on top of mine. He was hard everywhere, much bigger than me, and he smelled distinctly male—like sandalwood and musk. I could feel every contour of his body through the thin layers of fabric that separated us, could feel his heart slamming behind his ribs, almost as fast as mine.

Our faces were mere inches apart, and his amber eyes locked with mine, his long lashes dipping as he stared at me.

Then the moment broke.

The man rolled off me, ejecting the clip from his handgun as he did. He reached into his back pocket then jammed another clip into the weapon. Another shot hit the exam table, sending up a loud metallic ringing noise, and the man cursed.

I pulled my arms and legs in tight. I had no idea what was happening, why Doctor Shepherd had a gun, or who this man was, but my body instinctively made itself smaller, trying to avoid getting hit by a stray bullet.

Whipping his arm over the top of the exam table, the intruder let off another shot. A small rolling medical supply tray toppled as Doctor Shepherd threw himself away from the wall.

As the metal tray hit the floor with a clang, scattering needles, bandages, and antiseptic, the brown-haired man grabbed my hand, yanking me to my feet. He pulled me toward the door, laying down suppressing gunfire over my shoulder. I screamed and ducked—the gunshots had gone off so close to my head that my ears rang.

"Come on! I'll get you out of here!" he yelled. I saw his lips move, but his words sounded like they came from deep underwater, muffled and hazy.

Before I could even sort through what he wanted, we were running through the hall. The man had such a tight grip on my hand that I could barely feel my fingers, and I was in such a state of shock that it was all I could do to put one foot in front of the other. The siren continued to blare overhead, tearing through the air like a knife. The man shot the lock off a staff door and pulled me through, dragging me up a set of access stairs.

"Up here. Go! Go!"

My uncoordinated feet slipped halfway up, and I smashed my shin into the concrete stair, sending pain shooting up my leg. I fell down three steps and would've probably tumbled all the way back to the landing if the guy hadn't still had a death grip on me.

He hauled me up, still holding the gun in his other hand. My bare feet scrabbled at the concrete until I finally found my footing, and then we were running again.

On the next floor up, he shoved open the door with his shoulder, pointing the gun into the hallway as he whipped his head back and forth. It was empty.

This was a floor I'd never been on before. I hadn't even known it existed. It looked similar to the lab area below the main complex where I lived—what I'd seen of it, anyway. The hallway up here was clean and sterile, with tastefully decorated walls and marble floors. But the calming effect was destroyed by the alarm that seemed to blare even more harshly up here.

The man pulled me out of the stairwell and down the hall. His heavy boots rang loudly on the polished marble while my bare feet slapped a discordant rhythm. His grip on my hand finally loosened a bit, allowing me to wiggle my fingers. We passed an intersecting hallway, and I glanced down it as we hurtled by.

My breath stuck in my throat.

Mom.

I'd only caught a quick glimpse down the hall, but I was absolutely sure I'd seen her. My mom was here.

Without even thinking, I ripped my hand from the man's grasp. The action took him by surprise, which was probably the only reason I managed to break his grip.

He called out behind me, but I didn't hear him. I didn't even think about the fact that he very well might shoot me in the back as I ran away.

All I knew was that my mom was here, and I had to get to her.

I careened around the corner into the new hallway, my hospital gown flapping as I ran. My mom stood at the end of the hall where it met another corridor, and she looked up at the sight of me. Her brown eyes went wide behind her thick glasses. My heart clenched with a mixture of relief and worry.

I needed to get to her. I needed to tell her to get out of here.

Putting on an extra burst of speed, I raced toward her, a breathless cry rising to my lips.

She blinked twice then reached behind her, pulling something from the waistband of her jeans.

When her hands reappeared, time seemed to slow.

A gun.

My mom was holding a gun, its thick black grip resting easily in the palm of her hand. Her other hand came up to meet it, cradling the butt of the gun as she steadied it, bringing it up to aim straight at me.

My feet skidded on the slippery marble floor as my body tried to reverse its forward trajectory too fast, and I went down hard on my ass. A shot rang out, and my blood turned to ice. A bullet whizzed over my head, exactly where my torso had been just a second earlier.

Shock overtook me.

I couldn't move.

I couldn't breathe.

Mom. What are you doing?

She began to walk toward me, bringing down her arms a bit to aim the barrel toward my head.

I stared at it. Saw the small hole at the end where a bullet would burst forth to end my life. Saw the clean, dark lines of the metal, the gentle but firm way she held it in her grip. Her arms were braced, locked out in front of her, and her lips were set in a thin, firm line.

Behind her glasses, her eyes were unreadable.

Fear lanced through me, but it couldn't break through the haze of shock and confusion. I scrabbled backward on my butt like a crab, my hospital gown twisted and askew. But I wasn't moving fast enough. There was nowhere to go. My mom took another step forward, adjusting her grip on the gun slightly—

A figure burst into the hallway from the intersecting corridor behind her.

Before she could turn toward him, he tackled her, bringing her down with a loud yell and a grunt. My mom was tall and stocky, much bigger than I was, but the man had several pounds of muscle on her. He had dark skin and short hair, and his broad face was contorted in concentration as he and my mom wrestled for control of the gun in her hand.

"*Mom*!"

Heart burning, I made an arrested move toward them—to help her? Or to help the new stranger?—but before I could act, the man tore the gun from my mom's grip. In one swift movement, he brought the butt of it down against the side of her head.

I heard the crack. *Felt* it down to the pit of my soul.

My mom's head whipped to the side, then she went still.

Her brown-gray hair half covered her face. Blood leaked from the wound at her temple, and her glasses sat askew. One of the lenses was cracked in a spiderweb pattern.

"Fuck." The large man, still straddling her, checked her weapon for bullets then shoved the clip back into the gun. He looked up, taking me in at a glance before shifting his gaze over my shoulder. "This turned into a real fucking shit show."

"Yeah. We need to get out of here. Now. Where are Noah and Rhys?"

The voice came from behind me, and when I turned to look, the man with the slightly bent nose and brown hair was striding quickly down the hall toward us, his gun still held at the ready.

"Downstairs," the black man answered. "Noah thought there might be one more restricted access area where Sariah could've been kept. But I don't think she's here, man. It's over."

"Agreed."

The men continued to confer, each keeping their gun aimed down one end of the corridor in watchful suspense.

But I stopped listening.

I couldn't stop staring at the prone figure of my mother. I had somehow ended up pressed against the wall, and I wanted to crawl toward her, wanted to make sure she was okay—but I couldn't get my body to move.

When I turned the corner and ran toward her, there had been no one else in the hallway with us. The brown-haired man hadn't been behind me then. I was sure of it. It'd been just me and my mom... and she'd shot at me.

She'd aimed right for my heart and fired.

I couldn't process that fact, no matter how many times my terrified brain shouted the words. Her face was still, and except for the blood oozing from her temple, she looked exactly like she did when she came to visit me and fell asleep on my couch after one of our long talks.

Finally, my body did move. Slowly, tentatively, I crawled toward her. My hospital gown got caught under my knees, and my smiley face underwear were probably showing, but I didn't even care.

My eyes were locked on my mom's chest, trying to pick up the rise and fall that would tell me if she was still breathing. I reached out for her slowly, but movement at the end of the hall made me freeze.

My body tensed, and I braced for more gunfire.

But none came.

"Rhys! Anything?" the man who'd tackled my mom called out.

"What does it fucking look like?"

Two new men jogged quickly down the hall toward us. The one who'd spoken had curly black hair pulled back in a ponytail and a dark scowl on his face. The other was...

"Cliff?"

The word stuck in my throat, half whisper and half croak, as my brain overloaded completely.

Cliff looked down at me. He wasn't smiling now, but even with the serious expression on his face and the gun in his hand, there was something about him that radiated warmth and kindness. He did a double-take when he saw me, his eyes widening.

The man who had burst into the exam room at the beginning of this nightmare shook his head at the black-haired newcomer. "Sariah's not here, Rhys. I'm sorry."

"You don't fucking know that!" Rhys argued. "She could be hidden somewhere! This place is a totally different setup than the San Diego complex. Maybe they've got her in a separate wing! Maybe—"

Cliff broke his gaze away from me and looked up at his

friend. "Jackson's right. I've been here for a month, and I haven't found anything like that. This place is run by a small staff, but they've definitely called for backup by now. If we don't get out soon, we're not getting out. Ever."

"But if she's here—!"

"Dude!" The burly black man grabbed a fistful of Rhys's shirt, getting into his face. "Let it go! She wouldn't want you to give up your life trying to get her out. And if you die here, you'll never find her. We'll try again. But right now, *we have to go.*"

Rhys's lips curled up in a snarl. The two men were almost nose to nose, their foreheads practically touching. For a moment, thick tension hung in the air between them, and I almost expected Rhys to swing his gun around and shoot the other man in the head. He looked mad enough to try it.

Then he blinked. His jaw ticked and his nostrils flared, but he nodded stiffly. "We *will* try again, West."

It sounded almost like a threat. But the black man—West—didn't seem to take it that way. He released his grip on Rhys's shirt and slapped him on the chest. "Always, brother."

I stared dumbly up at them all. I felt like I was watching an action movie, a spectator removed from everything around me. My body had gone numb, and the continuous shrill whine of the alarm felt like it had permeated my brain, like it would never stop.

"Come on, Scrubs. We'll get you out of here."

Cliff held his hand down to me. I blinked at it, my toes curling into the cold marble beneath my feet. I didn't want to go anywhere. I couldn't leave this place. I was sick—I needed to stay here to survive.

This all had to be some huge misunderstanding, some intensely vivid nightmare.

"We gotta go!" the man named Jackson called, shifting his gaze down the opposite end of the hallway and raising his gun.

The sound of pounding feet rumbled like thunder under the high pitch of the alarm, and a moment later, half a dozen guards dressed in tactical gear rounded the corner.

Fear iced my blood.

Whatever backup these four men had been worried about, it had arrived.

CHAPTER SIX

"Motherfuck—!"

That was all I heard before chaos erupted. Gunshots echoed in the confined space of the corridor, and a hand—I wasn't even sure whose—reached down, hauling me to my feet. I found myself surrounded by four large bodies, racing down the hall of this unfamiliar level of the Strand complex.

More shots sounded, even as we outraced the men behind us. One of the guys bringing up the rear of our group grunted, his footsteps faltering briefly.

"West? Are you hit?" Cliff called.

"Yup."

"You all right?"

"Yup."

The word was curt and unemotional, as if running down

a hallway getting shot at was something he did so often it wasn't worth remarking upon.

Who the hell were these men?

And what did they want with me?

My body was jostled between the large men as we careened around a corner. The one called Rhys kicked open a door and led us up another set of access stairs. This time I managed to keep my feet under me, but just barely. Cliff switched his grip on me to my elbow, steadying me.

We raced up three flights of stairs, ducking every time one of the men chasing us shot up through the stairwell. My breath came in sharp gasps by the time Rhys shoved open the door at the top landing, and Cliff pulled me through.

Light nearly blinded me.

I staggered, blinking in the sudden onslaught of sunlight. The air was warm and slightly humid, and the asphalt beneath my bare feet was hot.

Before I could fully absorb the fact that I was outside, we were moving again, running across a small parking lot toward a row of parked cars. I threw a look back over my shoulder. The building we'd emerged from was small and innocuous-looking. It was a single story structure made of plain brown brick. Nothing about it gave any hint of the levels it housed underground, beneath the surface.

As I watched, the door we'd exited through opened again.

The first man to emerge was huge, tall as a tree and muscled like a TV wrestler. His neck was as wide as his head, and his blond hair was cropped short. There was a hard look on his face, and when my gaze met his, my blood ran cold. I thought I knew everyone at the Strand complex, but I'd never seen this guy before.

If I had, I was sure he would've haunted my nightmares.

He strode toward us, raising his gun.

Before he could fire, I was yanked sharply to the side, bringing my attention back to my immediate surroundings. Cliff dragged me behind a large SUV, blocking us from the approaching guards. Jackson smashed out the driver's side window and unlocked the doors while West and Rhys shot around the front of the car, slowing our pursuers.

Yanking open the back door, Cliff picked me up and practically threw me inside. I landed on the soft leather seat and scrambled to sit up.

"Now would be a great time to show off those hot-wiring skills you always brag about!" Cliff called to Jackson, sliding in beside me and pushing my head down with a hand at the back of my neck.

"I'm working on it, I'm working on it." Jackson's voice was tense with concentration.

A moment later, the engine roared to life.

"Tires!" he yelled to the two men still outside the car.

I had no idea what that meant, but when I lifted my head a little, I saw the guy called West turn his gun toward the other cars in the parking lot. While Rhys continued to shoot at the guards, who'd taken cover around the side of the building, West systematically shot out the tires of all the vehicles around us.

Smart.

My numb brain was reduced to processing a single thought at a time. I couldn't comprehend the entirety of what was happening to me, the nuclear bomb that had just gone off in my simple, uneventful life. But I could see that these men worked well together. That they were resourceful and smart.

Jackson gunned the engine as Rhys and West piled inside. West climbed over the middle console to crawl into the front passenger seat as Rhys slammed the back door shut. Then we peeled out.

I snuck a peek behind us as we sped toward the parking lot's exit. The men in black tactical gear raced out from where they'd taken cover. Several of them looked at the cars with punctured tires, and a few shot after us. But the big blond man, who towered almost a foot above his compatriots, didn't waste time with either of those things. He turned and jogged purposefully around the far side of the building.

Were there other cars over there? What had he and his men arrived in?

Bullets ricocheted off the back of the SUV, and Cliff put his hand on the back of my head again. I stared at my bare feet as the men's shouts filled the car and a sudden left turn shoved Cliff's large, hard body against mine.

"Damn it! That fucking blond Arnold Schwarzenegger is behind us!" someone called.

"Hold on." Jackson's voice was grim, and the car turned wildly again, sending me sliding the other way. I clenched my eyes shut and gritted my teeth, willing myself not to vomit.

Another shot pinged off the back of the car, making my heart leap into my throat.

This isn't real. None of this is real.

Maybe the new meds Doctor Shepherd had given me were messing with my system, causing hallucinations. Maybe I was inside the complex right now being rushed into the ER. But then why were the smells of metal, gunpowder, and leather so strong in my nostrils? Why was the back seat of the SUV full of Diet Coke cans?

Would I really dream that up?

"You all right, West? Where'd they get you?" Cliff asked, his voice taut with concern.

"Bullet grazed my arm. I'm fine."

I lost track of the twists and turns the car took as we sped down the road, West calling out directions to Jackson. When I finally peeked out the window, I saw that we were in a rural area, with trees lining the sides of the road. Jackson made fewer sharp turns, but he never let up on the accelerator as the inside of the car settled into a tense silence.

Finally, the car shuddered slightly, slowing.

"Shit. Stupid fucking SUV driver didn't fill up their tank. We're almost out of gas," Jackson muttered. "We're about ten miles from our stash."

"Just as well. If we drove any closer, we'd risk leading them right to us." Cliff spoke beside me, his voice soft. He'd let up his hold on my head, but I remained bent over, curled into myself, as if by making myself as small as possible, I could escape my new reality. "It's better if we cover the last bit on foot."

The car lurched again, slowing even more.

"Not like we have any fucking choice." Jackson chuckled humorlessly.

With a final shudder, the car eased to a stop. The front doors opened, and I heard the passenger side door open too. A moment later, strong hands slid around my waist. Cliff tugged me gently out of the car after him. The gravel on the roadside bit into my feet, and when I stumbled, he swept me up into his arms.

I shut my eyes, burying my face in the warm blue fabric of his scrubs. He was the only one of the four guys who wasn't dressed in black, loaded down with weapons and ammunition, and somehow that made him slightly less terrifying. In my head, I could still pretend he was just "Cliff the cute orderly," not some kind of renegade soldier who'd kidnapped me in a blaze of gunfire.

"You just going to carry her the whole way?" West sounded slightly amused and slightly annoyed.

"Yeah, man. I am," Cliff shot back. "You think she's going to walk like this?"

"As long as it doesn't slow us down. If she slows us down, we leave her."

That was Rhys, and the hard edge to his voice made my blood run cold. He wasn't kidding.

Cliff didn't answer, but his grip on me tightened a little, and that small gesture was so reassuring I felt tears sting my eyes. At least one of these men didn't want me to die—not that any of them would truly be able to stop it. I'd been taken from the Strand medical complex, the one place I was cared for, where I was safe.

Outside, exposed to a barrage of unknown pathogens, how long would I last? How long before my body turned on itself again?

And this time, there would be no doctors to rush me into emergency care, no one to adjust my meds and monitor my vitals. Just four burly men who, no matter how well trained they were with weapons, likely didn't know a thing about medicine.

I'm going to die out here.

That thought scared me, but not as much as it should have. I didn't want to die—had spent all those years in the Strand complex fighting against death. But right now, in my numb, hollowed out state, struggling to push away the memory of my mother aiming a gun at my head, a small part of me welcomed the idea of oblivion. Of peace.

The men had started to move. My head jostled against Cliff's shoulder as he ran, moving swiftly through the woods with long even strides, as if he carried no burden at all.

After a while, a loud rushing sound reached my ears. Water?

Cliff's voice rumbled in his chest as he murmured, "Sorry, Scrubs. We gotta go in."

Before I could even form the words to ask what he meant, ice cold water touched my butt, soaking through my underwear and hospital gown immediately. I gasped and jerked in his arms, and he looked down at me apologetically as he waded deeper into the river.

"We need to move downstream a bit. Hopefully, it'll make our scent harder to pick up."

I had only a vague idea what he meant by that, but I didn't complain. Rhys shot me a glare out of the corner of his eye as he trudged through the water ahead of us, and I pressed my face back against Cliff's chest as the water rose higher up my body. My entire midsection was underwater, and occasionally my feet and toes dipped under too. Those parts slowly went numb, while angry goose bumps covered the rest of my skin, making my entire body ache.

We walked through the water for so long I lost track of time. By the time we emerged downstream, the light had changed around us. We were in a heavily wooded area, but the gloom wasn't just from the canopy overhead. The sun was setting.

And still, the men didn't stop.

They continued through the woods, exchanging quiet words from time to time. My damp gown clung to my body—as we'd waded through the river, the water had slowly worked its way up, soaking through even the fabric that wasn't submerged.

"There. Up ahead."

"Thank fuck."

Cliff's steps quickened, and I roused myself slowly, looking up in time to see a small shelter ahead of us. It looked very homemade, consisting of a brown tarp slung between several closely spaced trees. Leaves and twigs were scattered across the top of the tarp, some hanging over the sides. Several large packs rested at the bases of the trees.

We walked beneath the tarp, which dipped slightly in the middle but was high enough to allow the men to stand upright. Cliff lowered me gently to my feet, and I staggered away from him like a baby deer. It was hard to stand—I was cold and exhausted and so emotionally strung out, I felt high. The world dipped and swayed in my vision, but I gritted my teeth, fighting to remain upright.

For a moment, the five of us just stood in silence. A bird called in the distance.

Then, suddenly, the black-haired man named Rhys roared.

As if he'd held back his emotions for too long, he unleashed a feral yell, a torrent of angry curses streaming from his lips. Turning, he struck out at a nearby tree trunk, smashing his fists against it until his knuckles were raw and bloody.

I'd never seen someone so violently angry in all my life. Unconsciously, I shrank away from him, bumping into a muscled chest behind me. Strong arms with dark skin wrapped around me, but before I could extricate myself from West's grip, Rhys rounded on me. His piercing blue eyes flashed with rage—and pain. Such a deep, soul splintering pain that the sight almost called tears to my own eyes.

He dragged me from West's grip, his bloody fingers

leaving red streaks on the damp fabric of my sleeves. He shook me roughly, his lips curling back in a snarl.

"Where is she? Sariah! Was she there? Did they kill her? Answer me!"

My brain rattled in my skull as he shook me again, and nausea churned my stomach.

"What the fuck did they do to her? What did *you* do?" His broad chest rose and fell quickly, and he gripped my arms so tight it hurt. "*Where is she*?"

"I—" My tongue felt thick, my lips numb. My teeth chattered uncontrollably. "I d-don't—know what you're—t-talking about. I didn't do—"

Cliff stepped forward, his gray eyes flashing. He shoved his friend away from me. "She didn't do anything, Rhys! Come on. Does she look like a fucking lap dog to you? She's as innocent as any one of us."

Without missing a beat, Rhys rounded on him. "Oh yeah? Then why was—"

But the rest of his angry words were swallowed up by the dull roar that filled my ears. My body shivered so hard it began to shake convulsively, and my knees buckled.

Oh no.

This was it.

My body had been strained to the breaking point, and my disease, having lain in wait for so long, would finally swoop in to finish me.

Please, God. Just let it be quick.

CHAPTER SEVEN

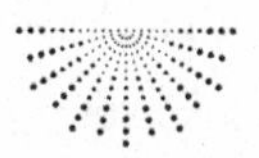

Strong hands caught me before I crumpled to the ground. I watched Rhys stare at me with malevolent, icy eyes as Cliff and Jackson lowered me gently to the ground.

"Jesus fuck! She's freezing." Cliff bit his lip. "Damnit, Scrubs, why didn't you say anything?"

"I'm n-not c-cold. I'm s-sick."

"You *are* cold. And wet. Shit, your fingers are like ice."

Cliff grimaced, wrapping his large hand around one of mine. My numb fingers could barely feel the pressure of his grip.

Rhys backed up a few paces, his expression a mixture of guilt, anger, and pain. Then he turned and raced off into the woods.

"Rhys!" Jackson called, looking up from where he knelt at my feet.

My toes peeked out from between his hands, almost blue in the waning light. Tremors still wracked my body, making it hard to speak, hard to breathe.

"Let him go. He needs to shift, he'll feel better after he does." West stared after Rhys, grimacing.

"We need to get some dry clothes on her." Cliff jerked his chin toward one of the packs set against a tree trunk. "West, grab that bag. The clothes we brought for Sariah should fit her."

"Oh, man." Jackson shook his head, a humorless chuckle falling from his lips as his hands rubbed my foot in a quick motion. "Rhys is gonna fucking love that."

"Well, someone should use them, right?" Cliff shot back. "And she's not here, is she?"

"Not arguing. Just sayin'."

I tried to follow their conversation, but all I could focus on were the strong, calloused fingers bringing life back to my hands and feet. My muscles still contracted involuntarily, but as Cliff and Jackson massaged my chilled skin, some feeling began to return to my extremities.

West dropped the large backpack on the ground next to me and squatted down, rifling around inside it. "Here. Got pants and a shirt, and socks and shoes. I don't know shit about sizes, but they look like they'll fit."

Hovering above me, Cliff met Jackson's eyes. "Do you want to...?"

"Undress her? What do I look like, a fucking lech?"

"Jesus Christ. Move." West elbowed Jackson away from my feet, and he and Cliff helped me sit up. He cupped the sides of my face, his large hands surprisingly gentle. "Listen, we've got to get you into warm clothes, okay? We're gonna take your gown off. There's nobody else in these woods, and none of us will look. We promise. Is that all right? Jackson will stand guard."

I jerked my head up and down quickly. If my body was attacking itself from the inside, a fresh set of clothes wouldn't do much to save me from death. But I craved warmth on a primal level, and at this point, I didn't care who saw me naked in the process.

"Okay. Pants first."

West grabbed the pair of pants and helped me work my feet through each leg. When they were bunched up around my thighs, he and Cliff leveraged me to my feet—although without the two of them holding me up, I wouldn't have stayed vertical. He slid the pants all the way up, reaching under my wet hospital gown to work them over my hips.

When he moved to pull the zipper up, a small breath escaped my lips.

I'd never been touched by any man as intimately as I'd been touched by these men today. It felt foreign and strange, but not altogether unpleasant. Despite the haze of confusion and fear, and the illness ravaging my system, I registered each touch as if they were mapping out uncharted places on my body.

When West slipped the top button closed, his gaze rose

to meet mine. Heat flickered in his dark eyes, and his voice was low when he spoke.

"Now the shirt."

I nodded, suddenly aware of how stiff my nipples were beneath the cold, wet gown. It clung to my body, the translucent fabric revealing so much I might as well be naked already. I had an urge to clamp my hands over my breasts, but instead, I remained perfectly still as West held me up with a firm grip on my hips and Cliff untied the back of the gown.

Then they switched. Cliff supported my weight while West slid the gown off my arms. I could tell he was trying to keep his promise, but for the briefest moment, his gaze flicked to my chest.

I swallowed, a confusing mixture of emotions swirling through me as my skin reacted to his look as though it were a physical touch.

The muscled black man cleared his throat and averted his gaze, tugging the shirt down over my head before helping me slip my arms through and pulling it down the rest of the way.

He seemed to relax as soon as I was fully dressed, and it was only then that I realized how tense he'd been before—as if he'd been holding himself in check somehow.

They lowered me down to sit on the ground, and I found myself cradled between Cliff's legs, my back pressed to his front. His clothes were still damp from the river, but he radiated so much body heat, I hardly cared.

"Uh, you guys look like you got this." Jackson glanced over his shoulder from where he'd been keeping lookout. "I'm gonna go find Rhys. Make sure he doesn't do anything stupid."

"Good idea," Cliff told him. "We don't need him howling all night. Keep him calm. And stay close."

"Yeah." Jackson stepped out from under the protection of the tarp. Then he paused and turned back, glancing down at me. "Hey, what's your name?"

I blinked, my brain so foggy I almost forgot the answer for a second before I whispered, "A-Alexis."

He nodded, regarding me thoughtfully. He looked like he smiled a lot, but he wasn't smiling now. "Alexis. Welcome to the pack. I'm glad you're okay."

I didn't respond, and after a second he shot me a lopsided grin. He gave a quick salute to the other two men before disappearing into the woods.

Where was he going? Where had the angry one with curly black hair gone? I didn't understand what was going on, and I found myself oddly concerned about the strangers who had abducted me.

Why should I give a single shit what happens to any of them? Is this what Stockholm syndrome feels like?

Maybe it was, but at the moment, I wasn't sure I cared.

West grabbed my feet, working them over with his hands just like Jackson had done, while Cliff draped his arms over mine, completely enveloping my fists in his larger ones. Warmth finally began to sink back into my bones, and my body stopped shuddering.

But as the cold slipped away, so did the last of my strength.

My eyelids drooped, and nothing I did could force them open again.

"I can't stay out here. I'm... sick..." I murmured, clinging to consciousness. They needed to know. They needed to understand. "I have to... go back. I don't want to die."

West made a sound low in his throat. The movement of his hands slowed, and he squeezed my feet in his warm grip.

Cliff let out a deep breath. His words tickled my ear as he spoke in a quiet voice.

"You're not sick, Scrubs; you never were. We won't let you die." There was a beat before he spoke again. "And you can't ever go back there."

CHAPTER EIGHT

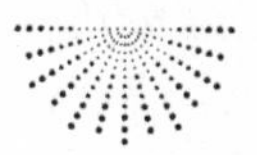

In my dream, I saw my mother's face.

She sat on the couch in my small room at the Strand complex, talking and laughing with me like we always did. Behind her thick glasses, her dark brown eyes were warm and open.

Sweet.

Loving.

And then they changed.

The light behind her eyes went out, and those once-kind windows to her soul became as blank and empty as black holes. And as the light inside them dimmed, the rest of her expression shifted too, the soft wrinkles on her face hardening to cold lines. One corner of her mouth lifted in a slight sneer as she reached behind her, pulling a gun from her purse and aiming the barrel right between my eyes.

Cold steel pressed against my forehead. But I knew it would be scalding hot after the gun fired.

After the bullet pierced my brain.

The barrel would smoke, and blood would splatter, and my life would end in a single loud bang.

My mom tilted her head to the side, regarding me where I sat frozen in fear.

"I wasted too many years of my life pretending to love you, Alexis."

Her voice wasn't the same. Nothing was the same. The woman I loved, who'd comforted me when I was sick, who'd visited me every week without fail—who had uprooted her life to be near me while I underwent treatment—was gone.

The person sitting across from me was a monster wearing my mother's face.

Hot tears blurred my vision as they spilled from my eyes, streaming down my cheeks and dropping off my chin.

"Mom." I drew in a shuddering breath, trying to push my fear and grief away. I needed to reach her somehow, to find the sweet woman under the cruel mask. She had to be in there somewhere. "I love you. Please, don't do this. I love you!"

She squinted, and suddenly the eyes behind the thick glasses were blue and slightly bloodshot.

Doctor Shepherd.

"No," he said. The glasses disappeared, and he stared down the barrel of the gun at me. His voice was as smooth and calm as ever. "You don't, Alexis. You only think you do."

Then he pulled the trigger, and my world blew apart.

~

I JERKED AWAKE, a scream tearing from my throat.

"Jesus! Keep her quiet!"

Before I could process where I was, a large body rolled over mine and a calloused hand covered my mouth. My shriek died in a muffled whimper, and I fought against the body pinning me down, jerking and kicking.

"Hey, Scrubs, it's okay! It's just me. It's okay!"

The whispered words penetrated my brain, and I blinked up at a pair of beautiful gray-blue eyes.

Cliff.

My muscles relaxed slightly. It was stupid; I had no reason to trust this man, or any of his friends. But with the horror of my dream still lingering on the edges of my mind, I needed something to cling to. I shuddered, letting out a broken sob, and the large man sat up, bringing me with him and wrapping his arms around me.

"It's okay, Alexis. We've got you. It was just a bad dream. We've all had them."

He continued to murmur a stream of comforting words into my ear, and I let him rock me gently until my heart rate slowed and my breathing evened out. As I grew calmer, I became uncomfortably aware of how much of our bodies were touching—and memories of the last time he'd touched me flooded my mind.

I wasn't uncomfortable with my body. I'd been sick for so long I was used to being poked and prodded by doctors, used to clinical stares. But I wasn't used to hands that touched me like I was a person, eyes that grew heated when they looked at me.

Clearing my throat, I pulled away from the blond man's embrace. He released me easily, and I scrambled back a few feet, kneeling on the soft ground beneath the canopy of the tarp as my gaze flicked back and forth between him and the tall black man called West. Early morning light pierced the branches of the trees in the forest, dappling the ground with speckles of yellow.

"Cliff." My voice was scratchy, and I tried to wipe my tears and snot away in a subtle movement—not like they didn't know I'd just been crying. "What... what is going on? Who are you?"

He grimaced slightly, looking a little sheepish. "Well, first of all, my name isn't Cliff. It's Noah."

I blinked. "What?"

"Cliff was the name I gave Strand when they hired me. I had a whole fake ID set up for their background checks and stuff."

"Noah," I repeated slowly, trying not to freak out.

This shouldn't be the thing that tipped me over the edge of sanity. Of all the strange events in the past twenty-four hours, this didn't even make the top ten. But why couldn't *anything* I believed stay constant for more than a few hours anymore?

I turned to the other man. "And what's *your* real name?"

He grinned, his full lips spreading wide over gleaming

white teeth. His features were beautiful, almost impossibly symmetrical, and two dimples graced his cheeks.

"It's still West. Noah was the only one who went in undercover, so he's the only one who got an alias."

"I don't understand. Went in undercover? Why? What were you doing at the Strand complex? Why did you kidnap me?" I paused, realizing that although I was cold and sore, I basically felt okay. "How did you treat me? Do you have medicine?"

Cliff—*Noah*—shook his head. "Nah. I mean, I think we have some painkillers in one of these packs. But you don't need medicine, Scrubs. I told you, you're not sick."

Jesus. Men.

I bristled. "You're going to tell me whether I'm sick or not? Do you realize how messed up that is? I've been dealing with Speyer's Disease since I was a kid, I think I would know—"

"You're not sick. You're an experiment."

His quiet voice cut off my tirade. The word *experiment* pierced my heart, spreading a dull ache in my chest. I had always worried about being seen only as my illness, as nothing but a walking medical mystery.

"No. I'm more than that. Doctor Shepherd said they're all invested in my recovery. They want to see me get better."

"They want to see you shift," West threw out, raising one eyebrow.

I furrowed my brows. "Shift?"

Instead of elaborating, he turned to Cli—*Noah*. "Her wolf hasn't been called yet?"

Noah scrubbed a hand through his hair, sitting back on his heels and regarding me. "No, not yet. They were doing something different with her. It was a smaller operation, fewer test subjects. They didn't talk much around me, since I was just an orderly, but they were all really interested in her progress. You saw how it was—that whole complex existed just to house a few subjects. And she was definitely their most promising one."

Anger and fear welled inside me, making me unusually bold.

"I'm not a fucking test subject! My name is Alexis Maddow, and I'm a human being."

The two men exchanged a glance I couldn't interpret before West looked back at me. "Yeah... that's not exactly true anymore."

"What. Are. You. Talking. About?"

I couldn't tell if they were giving me half-answers because they thought I couldn't handle whatever they had to say, or if they were deliberately trying to keep me in the dark.

All I knew was that I needed someone to say something that made sense before I entirely lost my shit.

I wasn't sure anymore what was going on at the Strand Corporation. I didn't know what had happened to my mother, why she had turned on me—and that wound was still so raw it hurt to even think about. And I didn't understand how I'd been outside for almost twenty-four hours, tromping through woods and streams, no less, yet seemed to be in okay health.

West must've read the look on my face, because he dropped the kid gloves. His voice was a little harder when he spoke next, and he didn't couch his words or speak in riddles.

"The Strand Corporation is a multi-billion-dollar biomedical research firm. For the past thirteen years, they've dedicated a large part of their operation to a secret project: creating shifters. People who are part human, part animal, able to take the form of both. They haven't perfected it yet. We don't know what they're trying to accomplish with this in the long-term, but they're still running tests. The complex you were in? All the 'patients' who were there? You were all a special batch of experiments."

I wanted to laugh. But the look on his face was so serious, his tone so somber, that I couldn't. So I didn't say anything. I just stared at him, as though if I waited long enough, maybe he'd take it all back.

Noah dipped his head to the side, catching my gaze. "It's true, Scrubs. We all came from another, now defunct complex near San Diego. We escaped a while back, and eventually they shut down that branch. But they didn't stop experimenting. Why would they? They're playing god, and it's working."

Finally, a small, incredulous laugh did burst from my throat. "No! That's crazy! I'm sick. I'm not an... an *animal*. I've never *shifted* in my life. That's fantasy stuff!"

"Yeah, but that doesn't mean it's not true." Noah's large

fingers dug lightly into the dirt by his side as he regarded me. "That night you seized? That was the shift starting to happen. Like I said, they did something different to you. A different dose, maybe a different cocktail of drugs? I'm not sure. But your change is coming. They were all really excited about it—that it was finally happening. I don't think anyone else at that complex survived their first shift."

A trickle of fear dripped down my spine as I remembered the other patients who'd been housed at the Strand complex with me. Now that I thought about it, I realized I'd been the longest-term resident there. Others had come and gone; I'd been told some of them got better and some of them didn't.

But if what these men were saying was true, none of them had been sick.

And none of them had gotten better.

They'd all died.

My throat tightened. I couldn't keep letting panic get the best of me like this, but I felt like I was trapped in a rushing river, smashing into rocks and boulders as I careened helplessly toward a fate I couldn't see or understand.

Disbelief warred with a growing, grim certainty.

Even if these men were lying, I could no longer deny one truth. Something had been very wrong at the Strand complex. I hadn't seen it because I hadn't wanted to—I'd been so focused on my hope for the future, on following Doctor Shepherd's orders so that my body could heal itself.

I hadn't seen it because the one person I thought I could trust more than anyone, my mother, had showed up every week to reassure me. She had placed absolute faith in the Strand Corporation and had urged me to do the same.

The enormity of the betrayal, of the lies that had surrounded me every minute of every day for the past ten years of my life, suddenly bore down on me like a thousand pounds of rubble. I leaned over, going to my hands and knees, and retched into the grass. I hadn't eaten anything since before my checkup with Doctor Shepherd yesterday—an event that seemed to have taken place in another lifetime—so all that flew out of my mouth was bile and spit.

Instead of yelling at me for barfing inside their little shelter, the two men sat sympathetically, letting me heave until my stomach was completely empty. My dark brown hair fell down around my face like a curtain, and as I gathered it up with a shaking hand, I felt Noah's hand on my back.

"I'm sorry, Scrubs. We didn't come there for you, but when I saw you in that hall, so scared and alone, I couldn't just leave you there. None of us could. Maybe it would've been kinder to let you live the lie a little while longer. But you would've found out eventually. Once you finally shifted, the life you were living would've been over."

I closed my eyes, trying to calm my racing heart as his words washed over me. My stomach still churned, but there was nothing left inside it. My heart felt just as empty too. I'd spent the past ten years living a simple, isolated life. Even though I hadn't had much, I'd convinced myself I had everything I needed.

But I never truly had anything. And now I have even less than that.

In a moment of painful, stunning clarity, I realized the four men who had stolen me away from the Strand complex were now my only lifeline in a world that loomed too large and dangerous to comprehend.

Blowing out a deep breath, I sat back, lifting my head. Noah's face was close to mine, his cloud-gray eyes dark with concern.

"You said..." I licked my dry lips. "You said *shifters*. Part human, part animal. What does that mean?"

He opened his mouth to reply, but movement in the sunlight-dappled woods caught his attention.

As if called by our voices, two large wolves prowled through the trees toward us.

CHAPTER NINE

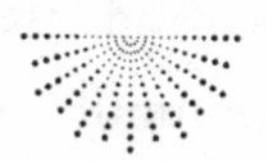

They were huge.

I'd always assumed dogs and wolves were basically the same. Not that I'd seen many of either, except for in movies or TV shows. But these wolves were massive, with thick fur and huge paws. One was pure white, and one had gray markings.

They padded closer, dipping their heads to sniff the ground. The white one with amber eyes looked right at me, and I found myself rooted to the spot. There was something intelligent and assessing—almost human—in his gaze.

West and Noah didn't seem the least bit concerned. They didn't even flinch as the two large wolves slipped inside the makeshift shelter.

I'd seen nature shows where rabbits or other prey animals froze in place when they sensed a predator, and I'd never understood where that instinct came from. But I understood it now. My body was rooted to the spot, torn between conflicting impulses to run, hide, or fight.

The gray wolf shook out his fur, and then...

He changed.

His entire body seemed to ripple. Bones shifted beneath the skin, changing size and shape. His fur retreated, vanishing into his body until only lightly tanned skin remained. Dark hair grew on his head as his face morphed from that of a wolf to that of a man.

The black-haired man named Rhys. The one who'd run off the previous night.

Beside him, the white wolf shuddered as well, and even before the change was complete, I knew who it would be.

Jackson.

Shifters. They were shifters.

My mind reeled. I'd seen the change happen right before my eyes, and I still could hardly believe it. West and Noah hadn't lied to me—about any of it.

The four of them were wolf shifters.

And at the moment, two of them were also completely, bare-ass naked.

My fear at being approached by two large predators splintered into a thousand other emotions. Shock. Awe.

Embarrassment.

Neither of the men paused in their stride or made any effort to cover their nudity. Jackson walked over to one of the packs that leaned against a tree-trunk, while Rhys came to a stop in front of me.

I tried. I did. I really and truly tried not to stare at the thick piece of muscle that hung between his legs, but since I was sitting on the ground, it was essentially at my eye level. And the harder I tried not to look, the more my eyes seemed to bug out of my head.

"What? You've never seen a naked man before?" Rhys cocked a challenging eyebrow at me.

No. As a matter of fact, I hadn't. I knew it was late in life to have missed out on something like that, but I'd never even been kissed, let alone gotten to second, third, or fourth base.

But I'd be damned if I was going to admit that to him. I was off-center, completely uncertain about where my life was going to take me from here on out. But one thing I felt certain of was that I couldn't let these men think they were better or stronger than me. I couldn't let them think I was weak. Couldn't let them know how inexperienced I was in so many ways.

"It's not that." I dragged my gaze up to his face before pointedly dropping it back down to his dick again. "I've just never seen one so small."

There was a moment of stunned silence as Jackson stopped digging through the bag by the tree. Then all three of the other men howled with laughter. I smirked, relishing my victory and somehow pleased to have lightened the mood in the camp.

Or at least, some people's moods.

Rhys's blue eyes chilled, and he raked his gaze over my body, taking in my shirt and pants. Sometime while I was asleep, the guys had put the socks and boots on me too. They were a little snug, but I'd take pinched toes over numb ones any day.

"Nice clothes," he said in a hard voice.

Noah's laughter died out. "Hey, I'm sorry, Rhys. But wherever Sariah is, she'd want Alexis to have them. You know that."

Rhys didn't answer. Sadness flitted across his features, almost as acute as I'd seen last night. Did he carry this pain everywhere with him? All the time?

Brushing his black curls away from his face, he turned away from me and joined Jackson by the tree. The two men stepped into fresh sets of clothes, then Jackson pulled out two pairs of boots, tossing one to Rhys.

Sympathy tugged at my heart. Whatever grief he carried, I could understand it. My wounds were still fresh, but I had a feeling they would never stop aching.

"I'm sorry." I hugged my arms around myself. "I don't know who Sariah is, but... I'm sorry I'm here instead of her."

"It's fine."

Rhys's voice didn't match his words at all, and he wouldn't look at me.

I tried again. "Whoever she is, I'm grateful to her."

"Sariah's his sister. She was held at the same complex we were in—" West began, but Rhys turned on him with a growl.

"Don't talk about her! *She*"—he jerked his head at me, lip curling—"doesn't need to know."

Jackson sighed, flopping down on the ground and leaning

against the tree trunk to tie his boots. "Come on, man. Don't be a dick."

"I'm not being a dick," Rhys ground out. "And this is not part of our plan. It isn't anywhere close to the plan. We should've gotten Sariah out and been halfway to New York by now."

"Yeah, but she wasn't there," Jackson countered. "So that part of the plan was already shot. What were we supposed to do?"

"Not pick up some stray who's only going to slow us the fuck down! We need to start planning a new strategy. We need to go back!"

West scrubbed at his short black hair. "She's not there, Rhys."

"Then I'll find out where she is! And I'll get her out myself if I fucking have to."

The other three men shared a look, and I had a feeling they'd had this discussion, or something like it, many times before. Rhys didn't seem like the type of man who gave up on an idea easily. And he clearly didn't give up on someone he loved easily.

I would've admired those qualities, if I didn't already sort of hate the moody, coldly handsome man.

"You won't have to do it alone," West finally said. "We're with you, brother. Always."

He stood, coming eye-to-eye with Rhys. All the men towered over me, but those two were the tallest. West had slightly broader shoulders than Rhys, and even through his long-sleeved shirt, I could see his muscles rippling as he moved. His left sleeve was torn and streaked with blood from where the bullet had grazed him.

"He's right." Noah stood, offering a hand and pulling me to my feet too. Jackson rose too, grumbling something about having just sat down. "We're with you. But we can't go back there. My cover is blown. They know all of our faces. Hell, they probably have hunters out searching for us right now. We can't just run back into the belly of the beast. We need to regroup, reorganize. And we need more backup."

"What? *Her*?" Rhys shot me a scathing look.

"My name's Alexis, not *her*." I tugged my hand out of Noah's. It was too comforting, and I couldn't allow myself to think of any of these men as my protectors, no matter how tempting it was. "And don't worry, I won't burden you. I'll..."

I trailed off. What the hell *would* I do?

I had no idea where I was. No clue how to navigate the world outside the Strand complex. Especially not on the run. And especially not as a... shifter.

"No way, Alexis. We got you out of that place. What kind of assholes would we be if we just abandoned you now?" Jackson smirked, raising a pointed eyebrow at the black-haired shifter next to him.

Rhys's stormy blue eyes narrowed, but he had the decency to look a little ashamed.

"You can come with us," he said grudgingly, and I had to bite my lip to keep from throwing the offer back in his face.

As mad as he made me, I couldn't afford to wander off on my own in a huff.

Instead, I nodded, lowering my eyes. "Okay."

"That still leaves the question, where the hell are we going?" Jackson cocked his head, staring off into the woods and listening intently.

The movement was so animalistic that for a moment, I vividly remembered the white wolf who'd padded into the makeshift enclosure a few minutes ago. It was still there, under the surface of Jackson's skin. I never would've noticed or believed it if I hadn't just seen him shift, but now that I knew it existed, I could sense the animal inside him.

Was something like that really inside me too? Right now, I almost wished it were true. I longed for the strength of an apex predator, the instincts and power of a wild wolf.

But all I could sense inside myself at the moment was a very scared, very confused human.

"I dunno, but we need to get moving soon." Noah followed Jackson's gaze, his large, warm hand enfolding mine again. "I don't know how many resources Strand will dedicate to hunting us, but that blond Terminator dude definitely looked like he meant business. And the fact that we stole their prize experiment..." He looked back at me, a surprisingly protective glint in his eyes. "Yeah, they'll be coming after us."

My stomach dipped. Less than twenty-four hours ago, I would've been thrilled to return to the Strand complex. But now? A shiver of fear raced down my spine at the prospect.

"What about the Lost Pack?" West hefted a large backpack over his shoulder, his dark eyes serious.

"We don't even know they exist. It could just be a rumor." Rhys looked torn between hope and despair.

"What's... the Lost Pack?" My voice was soft. I was half-afraid Rhys would bite my head off again.

But he surprised me by turning to me and answering, his tone less openly hostile than it had been before. "The Strand Corporation has been doing experiments on humans for years. When they started the shifter initiative, I don't think they really knew what to expect. Their security wasn't nearly as good as it should've been, considering what they created. In the early days, a lot of the shifters escaped, and rumor has it, a group of them formed a pack in the Pacific Northwest." He shifted his gaze to West. "But we don't know if it's true."

"Hey, man. Beats the fuck outta sitting around here waiting for Strand to come after us. And who'd be more likely to help us bust your sister out than shifters who've escaped themselves? They'll understand better than anybody." Jackson rocked on his feet, practically bouncing on his toes.

"That makes sense to me," I said tentatively.

I barely understood what was going on, and I doubted I'd get a vote in any of this. But Jackson's restless energy was rubbing off on me, and I was anxious to get moving. My gaze kept darting into the woods as if at any moment, I'd catch a glimpse of bright blond hair and hulking muscle.

Rhys regarded me so intensely it felt like he was trying to read my mind, to strip away all my defenses and see right down to my soul. His eyes were a startling blue, brighter than Noah's, like an infinitely bright blue sky.

I didn't blink, didn't look away, as his gaze devoured me.

"Is that what you want, Scrubs?" He used Noah's nickname for me, but it sounded different rolling off his tongue. Less affectionate and more like a quiet threat. "You want to meet more of your kind? More people like us?"

My heart was beating too hard in my chest. How did he—how did *all* of these men—put me off balance so quickly? I felt like a bumbling idiot around them, awkward and unsure.

But I nodded, forcing my chin up and down. "Yes. I do." I hesitated, then added, "And if they might be able to help get your sister back, that's a chance worth taking, right?"

He ran a hand through his wavy black hair. It'd been tied back in a low ponytail yesterday, but now the ends of the dark strands brushed his shoulders. Finally, he nodded decisively. "Like Scrubs says, it's worth a shot."

"Exactly what I said! Now quit eye-fucking her, and let's go." Jackson swiped a bag from the ground and set off through the forest, his laugh lingering behind him.

I flushed all the way from my toes to the tips of my ears, and to my surprise, Rhys's cheeks reddened a little too. He tore his gaze away from me, bending down to pick up the pack West had pulled Sariah's clothes from yesterday. He tossed the bag in my direction, and I hastily disentangled my hand from Noah's so I could catch it before it hit me in the chest. Noah made a sound low in his throat, almost like a growl, but Rhys ignored him.

"If you're coming with us, you're gonna have to pull your own weight, Scrubs. No free rides here. This isn't a fucking vacation," he said, before grabbing a pack of his own and heading off after Jackson.

And just like that, I was back to hating the moody asshole.

CHAPTER TEN

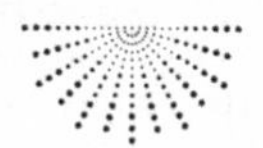

I stared after Rhys's retreating form, a riot of emotions banging around in my chest.

"Here, Scrubs. Let me help you."

Noah tried to take the bag from me, but I held onto it with an iron grip. "No! That's okay."

It was the same size as all the others and surprisingly heavy, but I refused to let Rhys be right about me—I wouldn't be a burden or a freeloader. I shoved my arms through the straps and hefted the backpack higher on my shoulders, following after Jackson and West. They trailed behind Rhys, hanging back to wait for us.

I hoped at least one of these guys knew where we were going, because I certainly didn't. I had a vague idea that east was behind us, where the sun hovered low on the horizon, but that was about all the sense of direction I possessed.

As we caught up to the two men, they parted to make room, and I found myself walking between them.

Jackson shot me a look out of the corner of his eye. "So, you must have about a million questions, huh?"

I thought about that for a second as we tromped through the underbrush. I did have questions, but there were so many it was hard to articulate any of them. And there were several I wasn't sure I was ready to hear the answers to. But if he was volunteering information, I shouldn't waste this opportunity.

"Yeah." I looked up at him, squinting against the morning light. "I guess I do."

"Then ask away. I'm an open book." He grinned. His nose had definitely been broken before, and with the teasing tilt of his lips, he looked dangerously handsome and wild.

I ripped my gaze away from his face before he could catch me staring, blurting out the first question that popped into my mind. "Does it hurt when you shift?"

He swept a low-hanging branch out of the way, pursing his lips thoughtfully. "A little. It hurt more the first few times, but now I'm just used to it. It's like if you crack your knuckles over and over—eventually you don't really feel it at all."

That didn't help calm my fears. One of the nurses at the Strand complex had cracked her knuckles, and the sound had always made me cringe.

"How long have you been able to do it?"

He cocked his head. "I shifted for the first time when I was twelve."

My brows shot up, and I almost twisted my ankle as I turned to look up at him. "Twelve? How old are you now?"

"Twenty-five."

"Thirteen years." I drew the words out slowly. He was four years older than me, and he'd been shifting for over a decade. If these men were right, and I was also a subject of the Strand's experiments, why hadn't I shifted once yet? Brushing off my sudden worry that there *was* something wrong with me, I glanced at West. "What about you?"

"My first shift? When I was fourteen."

"When did you escape Strand?"

Jackson glanced over my head to meet West's eyes before answering. "Six years ago. We all escaped together—the four of us. Been together ever since."

The look they shared made a sharp pain flare in my chest. It was just a casual glance, but it spoke of family, brotherhood, and love. I couldn't imagine what they'd been through in the past six years, or what they'd experienced before that either. But whatever it was, it had cemented the bond between all four of them more deeply than even blood could.

I wished I had something like that.

"I can't believe my mom just gave me up to the Strand Corporation like that," I murmured, realizing only after the words were out of my mouth that I'd spoken my deepest hurt aloud. My voice wavered as I fought to keep it under control. "She went along with everything they said, told me they'd take care of me. But... she knew. The whole time, she knew."

Jackson leaned toward me slightly, bumping my arm with his in an affectionate gesture. The brightness of his amber eyes dimmed a little as he looked down at me. "I hate to tell you this, Alexis, but that woman probably wasn't your mother."

My foot caught on a root, and I stumbled several steps, almost falling forward onto the soft ground. West caught my elbow, steadying me.

"She... she wasn't?" I whispered, my steps slowing.

Some part of me had realized that the moment she'd shot at me. Even if she had been my mother by blood, she was no longer a mom in any of the ways that counted.

Not if she could look me in the eye and aim a gun at me.

Maybe knowing she wasn't my real mom should've been reassuring—but it wasn't. It didn't change the fact that I'd loved her for as long as I could remember. It didn't change the fact that she'd lied to me my entire life. And it didn't change the fact that my real parents, whoever they were, had given me up somewhere along the line.

"No." It was West who answered, his grip on me tightening slightly as he spoke. "She was a Strand employee. They probably bought you on the black market or snatched you from the foster system when you were little. That's how they got most of the younger test subjects in our complex. Some of the older ones were homeless. People no one would miss."

"That's awful."

My stomach twisted with pity, until I realized *I* was also one of those people no one would miss.

"Yeah." Jackson's voice was hard as glass. "It is."

"But... I don't understand." I shook my head, adjusting the backpack slightly on my shoulders as I walked. The straps were starting to dig in, the weight of the bag bearing down hard on my back, but I pushed the discomfort away. "Why? Why go to all that trouble? I lived at the Strand complex for years. Since I was eleven. All my memories from before I got there are fuzzy, but I always thought that was because I was sick all the time. They must've done something to make me forget."

"Seems likely. It wouldn't be that hard, with the kind of pharmaceuticals they have access to." West nodded.

"But *why*?" I insisted. "That was such an elaborate setup, just to make me think I belonged there. Why do all that for me?"

"Because you're special, Scrubs," Noah said from behind me. "Something about you is different, and important."

"Yeah, they didn't do all those bells and whistles for us," West added, his voice tinged with anger. "They treated us like fucking dogs."

Special.

They'd used that word before. But I didn't feel special.

I felt alone, unwanted, and unloved.

Tears stung my eyes, burning hot trails down my cheeks. I blinked rapidly but didn't reach up to wipe them away. I didn't want to draw attention to the fact that I was crying. I didn't want to look as weak as I felt.

If the guys noticed, they didn't say anything, giving me time to process my grief privately. We lapsed into silence after that, the quiet stillness of the forest broken only by the crunch of our feet on the ground. With every step I took, I could feel myself getting farther and farther away from the life I understood.

I was walking into a great unknown, a vast, uncharted territory, and fear of the future felt like a lead weight around my ankles, making every step drag.

The backpack grew heavier and heavier on my back too. I wasn't in bad shape, thanks to the regimen Erin—or whatever the fuck her real name was—had created for me. But I wasn't used to being outside, wasn't used to functioning on too little sleep with too little food and water. The one break we took at midday was hardly enough to restore my flagging strength.

Don't be the weak link, Alexis. Don't give them a reason to leave you behind.

Those words became like a mantra over the next few hours, repeated over and over in my head as I forced one foot in front of the next—tripping over roots and rocks more often as my strength and coordination faded. But none of the men surrounding me showed any signs of tiring. So I gritted my teeth and kept going.

Until I couldn't anymore.

A wave of gray crept over my vision, and I pitched forward, landing on my hands and knees. My backpack slipped to one side, and the weight almost dragged me over. I dug my fingers into the dirt, fighting the dizziness that threatened to overwhelm me.

"Shit! Scrubs, are you okay?" Noah's face swam in my vision, his stormy blue eyes worried.

"Uh huh. I'm fine," I slurred, unconvincingly.

"Should've carried the damn pack myself," he chastised under his breath, helping me sit up and tugging the backpack off my shoulders. I suddenly felt so light I thought I might float away.

"What's wrong with her?" Rhys stood over me.

I hauled myself to my feet, the movement way too fast. I almost fell again. He reached out to catch me, but before he could touch me, I staggered away.

"Nothing. I'm fine." My voice was stronger this time. Pride and anger were giving my body the shot of adrenaline it needed. I would *not* allow Rhys to help me.

"Bullshit, you're fine." Noah picked up my pack, slinging one strap over his shoulder as if the combined weight of two bags was nothing. He turned to Rhys. "She's not used to this. She's still basically fucking human, not to mention she's been living inside a bunker. Shit, her wolf hasn't even been called yet. We can't just expect her to keep up with us. She needs a break."

"Goddamnit!" Rhys stalked a few paces away before coming back to stand in front of us. He clenched his hands into fists, and I noticed his knuckles were bruised and scabbed from his attack on that tree. "I fucking knew it! It's already happening. We're already changing everything for her! This isn't a fucking Disney cruise, and if she wanted it easy, she shouldn't have—"

"What?" Noah's voice was quiet. "Been abducted by Strand? Had her entire life stolen from her? Been ripped away from everything she thought she knew? None of us signed up for this, Rhys. All of us got a raw fucking deal. Remember that, or when we finally find Sariah, you won't be the brother she deserves."

Rhys stared at him, his jaw set. He swallowed hard, but didn't speak.

"We need to stop sometime soon, anyway," Jackson put in. "We've gotta snag a new ride. No harm in getting a little sleep while we're at it. It's a long way to Washington state."

Washington.

I wrapped my arms around myself as I processed his words. That was our final destination. Where the mysterious and possibly nonexistent "Lost Pack" resided.

And I was headed there with four men I barely knew. One of whom clearly hated me, and none of whom I was certain I could trust.

CHAPTER ELEVEN

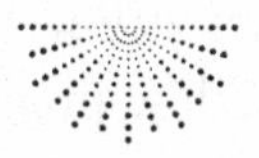

With a little more prodding from the other three, Rhys finally agreed it was a good idea to stop. I celebrated inwardly while remaining outwardly stoic. The truth was, I wasn't sure how much farther I could go before I fell over and couldn't get up again.

Fortunately, we weren't as far from civilization as I'd thought. Noah carried my pack as we trekked through the woods for another mile or so before emerging onto a small, two-lane road. Another ten minute walk led us into a small town that looked like its heyday had been several decades ago. Half the shops seemed to be closed up, and the paint on most of the buildings was faded and peeling. But I didn't care. The hotel on the outskirts of town had a sign out front that read "Vacancy," and I could already feel the softness of a pillow against my cheek, the comfort of a roof over my head.

"We shouldn't all go in," Jackson said as we walked down

the quiet street toward the hotel. "If four guys and a girl check into one room in a middle-of-nowhere hotel like this, they're definitely gonna think something shady is going on."

"We'll go." West grabbed my elbow, pulling me toward him. "You guys go get us some food."

The others nodded, splitting off silently. I wondered if their attempt at keeping a low profile was pointless. All four of these men were distractingly handsome, and in a small town like this, I was sure we stood out whether we wanted to or not. But I didn't voice my concern as West led me toward the old hotel. It was a two-story structure with a small parking lot out front. An office sat in the center, and two wings extending out and back from there. Room numbers were tacked to each of the doors.

West opened the door for me, gesturing me inside the small, dingy office. There was a coffee maker on a little table set near one wall, with a half a pot of what smelled like very burnt coffee sitting neglected inside it. Old magazines were placed in a loose stack nearby.

No one was behind the counter, but when the door slammed shut too hard between us, a voice called out.

"Coming!"

A middle-aged man with a trucker hat shoved over shoulder-length brown hair stepped out from the back room and leaned on the counter with both elbows.

"Hey there, folks. What can I do for you?"

"We need a room for the night," West answered, stepping up beside me.

The hotel clerk swept his gaze over the two of us, letting it linger on me. His thick tongue darted out to lick his lips as he cocked his head.

I'd gotten used to being poked, prodded, and observed at the Strand complex, where it was an almost daily occurrence. But no one had *ever* looked at me the way this man was staring at me now.

I hated it.

It made my skin crawl—made me feel helpless and dirty, even though I couldn't quite tell why.

The man tossed his stringy brown hair over his shoulder, grinning at me. "A room for the night, huh? What kind?"

"Double." West's voice had taken on a hard edge, and when I glanced over at him, I saw his jaw clench.

The man seemed pleased by that answer for some reason. "Huh. Not a single? Can't quite close the deal?" He winked at me. "You need a real man, honey? You just come find me."

He chuckled, still running his gaze up and down my body, as if he had every right to stare at any part of me he wanted for as long as he wanted. I shivered. I wanted to step back, to cower behind West. But the same instinct that had made me stand up to Rhys kept me still now.

Fuck that. I wouldn't run. I wouldn't let this man think he had power over me.

West's arm slid around my waist, his large hand resting gently on my hip. He didn't look at me though. His eyes were locked on the leering desk clerk, and I could practically feel the anger radiating from him.

"You heard what I said. We need a double. One night. How much?"

The man's attention went to my side, where West's hand curled possessively around my body. Then he flicked his gaze up to meet West's, his lip curling. "Sixty."

"Fine."

West pulled me forward, keeping his arm around me. He reached into his back pocket with his free hand and pulled out a small stack of bills. With a loud thunk, he slapped them on the counter. I had stiffened when he first drew me into his side, but now I tentatively returned the gesture, slipping my arm around his waist under the pack strapped to his back. It felt a little strange, and I wasn't sure where to put my hand. Finally, I reached around his front with my other arm and clasped hands, enclosing West in the world's most awkward hug.

The slimy desk clerk scowled, then rolled his eyes and grabbed the cash off the counter, turning to the wall behind him to grab a key card labeled 25. He chucked it toward West, then collected the—false—name the room would be rented under.

Finally, West steered me toward the exit, only releasing me from his grasp to open the door for me again.

We took a right and went up the stairs, following the upper walkway toward our rented room.

"Thank you for that," I murmured.

"No problem. You must get creeps like him eyeballing you all the time."

I huffed out a mirthless laugh. "Actually, no. He was the first. The doctors at the Strand complex might be mad scientists, but at least they never stared at me like that."

West's easy stride hitched, and he looked down at me with a grimace.

"Oh, shit. Right. I'm sorry." We reached our room, and he slid the key card into the lock. "Out here, it's probably going to happen a lot. With the way you look? Creeps will come out of the fucking woodwork for sure."

With the way I looked?

I'd never considered myself particularly attractive. I'd had a full-length mirror in my room at the Strand complex, and I'd sometimes stood in front of it, examining my naked body as though searching for weaknesses. Places where my disease might attack.

My legs and arms were toned and my stomach flat thanks to my work with Erin. I had a small, elfin nose that came to a delicate point, a heart shaped face, and high cheekbones. I'd always thought my eyes were my best feature—although now, remembering how closely my "mom's" had seemed to match them, I sort of hated the rich amber color.

I knew what all the individual parts of me looked like, but I'd never really considered what they all added up to. What my appearance was like to an outside eye.

A flush rose in my cheeks as I remembered the way West himself had looked at me the night before, when he'd helped me out of my hospital gown and into dry clothes. The way his gaze had slipped just for a half-second to take in the bare skin of my breasts. The heat in his eyes when he'd looked back at my face.

But the expression he'd worn then hadn't been anything like the look the hotel clerk had on his face. It hadn't made my skin crawl. Instead, it had ignited a small fire inside my belly that still seemed to burn low, flaring with sudden heat every time West touched me or looked at me with his deep brown eyes.

The hotel room door swung open, and for a moment, we just stood outside it. West's hand rested on the handle, but he made no move to enter the room. I was sure he could read every emotion on my face, and I tried to push down the blood coloring my cheeks by sheer force of will as I broke away from his gaze and stepped inside.

"This is nice."

I glanced around the small room. The carpet was aggressively orange, and chintzy watercolor paintings decorated the walls. Two large beds sat a few feet apart against one wall, and the rest of the space was mostly bare.

West chuckled. "No, it isn't. You really have been locked up too long, haven't you?"

The heat in my cheeks increased. "Yeah, I guess so."

I sat on the bed while West dropped his bag and prowled around the room. He checked the bathroom then switched on the lights and tugged the curtains on the window closed. He leaned casually against the wall between the door and the window, peeking out through the space between the curtain and the frame.

The room was quiet for a few minutes before the silence began to grate on me. I'd been used to days passing with minimal conversation at the Strand complex, but everything was different out here.

Silence was no longer comforting like it had once been. Now it was loaded with millions of unsaid things.

"Is Rhys okay?" I blurted.

West's eyes met mine, their dark depths soft and mysterious.

"Yeah, he will be." He crossed his arms over his chest, the muscles of his biceps bunching and bulging. "We had to leave his younger sister, Sariah, behind when we escaped the compound we were all being held in. She told him to go —*begged* him to—but he's been fucked up about it ever since, as you can imagine."

I bit my lip, pity for the ice-cold man filling my chest.

"He was so sure Sariah was in that complex where we found you." West rubbed the back of his neck. "It hit him hard. Now he's mourning her loss all over again."

My stomach twisted. "But she's not gone, right? I mean, she's still alive somewhere?"

West's face was impassive, but his voice was heavy. "We don't know."

His words settled between us, but before I could ask anything else, he whipped his head to the side, peering out the window again. He opened the door and waved outside, drawing the attention of the other three guys as they walked across the hotel's parking lot. They changed direction, veering toward the stairs.

When they were all inside the room, West kicked the door shut and slid the chain into place.

"We couldn't decide what to get, so we got some of everything." Noah dropped a plastic bag on the bed next to the one I was sitting on.

Jackson mimicked his movement, adding another bag and some bottles of water. "Yeah, we supersized the shit out of it."

The most enticing aroma I'd ever smelled drifted up to meet my nostrils, and drool pooled in the corner of my mouth. Without even realizing what I was doing, I stood and drifted over toward the other bed, eyeballing the large bags.

"Have you ever had fast food, Scrubs?" Noah asked curiously.

I shook my head, chewing on my lower lip.

"You can pick first, then. Whatever you want. And there's plenty, so go nuts." He grinned and stepped back, gesturing to the bed with a grand flourish.

I shot a quick glance at all the guys. Everyone but Rhys nodded encouragingly. He probably hated to see me getting special treatment again, but the rumbling of my stomach spurred me on despite his death glare.

Tentatively, like a squirrel sneaking up to a picnic, I crawled onto the soft mattress and reached into one of the bags. I didn't have the guts to rifle through it all, so I just grabbed the first thing I touched and unwrapped it.

A hamburger. I knew that much, although I'd never eaten one before.

Holding it in both hands, I took a small bite.

My eyes bugged out. *Holy shit. So fucking good.*

I chewed in a hurry before going in for a second bite that was twice as big as the first. The burger wasn't huge, and after just a few more bites, it was gone. I barely restrained myself from licking the paper it'd been wrapped in. Instead, I reached into the bag again and drew out a container of French fries, wolfing them down too.

Then I had another burger. And another.

By the time I finished, I was pleasantly stuffed. I hadn't realized how hungry I was. And I hadn't known how fucking delicious fast food was.

I was licking the salt from the fries off each of my fingers when I finally came back to my senses and realized the men were staring at me. My heart stuttered in my chest, and I looked up, eyes wide.

"Shit! I'm sorry. Did I take too much?"

They all looked slightly stunned as they took in the carnage of empty wrappers around me. Their expressions were a mixture of surprise, awe, and something else I couldn't quite pinpoint. Something that only made my blush deepen.

Then Jackson laughed, the infectious sound breaking the tension.

"Fuck no! That was amazing. I like a woman who isn't afraid to eat."

The other three chuckled, and I had a sudden desire to

melt into the carpet. I scrambled off the bed, gesturing to the bags. "Er, I'm done."

The guys descended on the remaining food, polishing it off in short order—although none of them ate quite as much as I had.

I watched them talk and bicker good-naturedly among themselves, wondering if I'd ever learn to act normal around these men. To become something more than a curiosity or an oddity to them.

And more importantly, I wondered why I cared.

CHAPTER TWELVE

I woke in a cold sweat.

Images of my mom had infiltrated my dreams again, along with strange and twisted visions of the Strand complex. Instead of being the safe haven I'd once seen it as, the walls in my dream had dripped with blood, and screams had echoed down the corridors as I was dragged into dark laboratories under the main building.

When my eyes popped open, a shout hovered on my lips. I choked it back, burying my face in the pillow as my body shook with latent fear. The pillowcase was wet, I realized, soaked with tears I didn't remember crying.

I dragged the blanket over my head and lay curled up beneath it for a moment, trying to block out the world.

When my heart rate finally slowed, I lifted the covers. The room was empty. With my belly full last night, I'd crawled into bed and passed out, exhausted from the long day. I hadn't even considered the sleeping arrangements, and as I peered around the dingy room, guilt rose up in me.

Blankets had been torn off the other bed, probably so some of the guys could sleep on the floor. They'd given me an entire bed to myself, and although I appreciated the gesture, I felt like a royal asshole.

Not that I want *to share a bed with any of them,* I reminded myself quickly. But I could've been the one to take the floor.

And where were they all now?

A sudden stab of panic pierced me. Were they gone? Had they decided Rhys was right about me being too much of a burden and abandoned me here?

I sat up, clutching the blanket to my body as my gaze scanned the room. Two of the packs were still here. The sight made my chest unclench just a little. They might leave me behind, but I seriously doubted they'd purposefully leave without their stuff.

Pushing down my fear, I threw the covers off and padded over to the backpack I'd carried yesterday. There were more clothes in it, including brand new underwear and a bra. In fact, everything in Sariah's bag still had tags on it.

These things were all new, probably bought by Rhys in anticipation of freeing his sister. My guilt about wearing her clothes piled on top of the guilt about hogging the bed, and I felt about as tall as an inchworm as I headed toward the bathroom to shower.

The Strand complex had been a prison in disguise, but it

was still hard not to miss certain things about it. Like the shower. Especially compared to this hotel's shitty shower, where huge droplets of water pelted me hard enough to sting, and the temperature knob balanced on a razor's edge between scalding and freezing. I spent the entire time adjusting the knob by eighths of an inch, and by the time I stepped out, my skin was pink from the wild temperature swings.

I threw on a fresh set of clothes and stepped out of the bathroom just as Noah and Jackson returned.

"Oh, hey, Scrubs. You're up!"

Noah kicked the door shut behind them with his foot, smiling at me—the same smile that had knocked my socks off the first time I'd met him.

A lot had changed since then. I now knew his name was Noah, not Cliff. I knew he was a wolf shifter, and I might be one too. In fact, my entire world had pretty much fallen down around my ears in the past few days.

But the effect his smile had on me was exactly the same.

My tongue immediately tied itself in knots, and I nodded awkwardly, settling onto the bed to roll up my old clothes and stuff them back into the bag.

"We brought some breakfast. Shit, I can't wait to see you decimate these," Jackson teased, dropping a box of donuts on the bed.

Oh geez.

I was never going to live that down. Jackson seemed to

find my voracious appetite for new foods both hilarious and—shockingly—attractive.

I peeked into the box. It looked like it'd once held a dozen donuts, although there were fewer than that now. Feigning nonchalance, I picked up a plain one dusted in cinnamon sugar and took a bite. Rich sweetness exploded on my tongue, and I worked hard to bite back a moan. The two men were already staring at me; I didn't want to make it any worse by adding pornographic noises.

To distract myself from wolfing down the entire pastry in two seconds, I looked up at them. "So, what's the plan? Where are you headed now?"

"*We're* headed to Washington," Noah answered, emphasizing the word *we* as he made a gesture that encompassed me. "But we need to make a quick stop on the way. We have an old friend who might be able to help us. West and Rhys are picking up a car right now."

My brow furrowed, and I quietly snuck another donut. Somehow, despite my attempts at restraint, I'd finished the first one while Noah was speaking. "From where? Is there a car rental place in this town?"

"Oh, Alexis." Jackson smirked at me, plopping down onto the bed next to me and stretching out his long, muscular form. "They're not renting a car. They're stealing one."

I almost choked on my donut.

Oh. I shouldn't have been surprised to hear that. After all, these same men had broken into the Strand complex two days ago and stolen something valuable from that place too—me.

But it was still hard to wrap my head around the fact that they were off stealing a car. It probably said a lot about how unworldly I was, but none of these guys fit what I imagined carjackers would look like.

Almost as if he could read my mind, Noah grinned at me. "Hey, when you're living under the radar, you take whatever work you can get. After we escaped the Strand compound in San Diego, we fell in with a crew in Vegas. Learned a lot of useful skills on the jobs we did. Not all of them legal," he added with a wink.

I found myself grinning back at him. My shock was beginning to fade, and for the first time since leaving Strand, I found myself feeling excited and a little hopeful. I didn't know if I'd ever get over the lies I'd been fed my entire life, but it was finally starting to sink in that I'd gotten the one thing I wanted most in the world: to *be in* the world.

This was real life, in all its messy, terrifying, unknowable glory. And as much as it sort of made me want to bury my head under the covers again, there was a part of me that relished it too. The bright chaos of the outside world was a constant reminder that I was alive.

That I was free.

That I'd made it this far.

"We all know how to hot wire a car. We could do it in our sleep. You didn't think the owner left the keys in that SUV yesterday, did you?" Jackson raised his eyebrows at me, leaning over the bed to grab a donut from the box.

He had a pleasant sandalwood scent that tickled my nostrils, and the proximity of his body to mine made the little hairs on my arms stand up. I wasn't used to having other people this close, let alone such unnervingly handsome men, and it threw me off balance.

"It's not really a two person job, but it's easier if there's a lookout." He shrugged. "Safer too. I'm sure the Strand Corporation is still trying to find us, and if we have to split up the pack, it's better to do it two-by-two than to send anyone off on their own."

I toyed with the second half of my third donut. "Pack. Right. That's what you guys are. It's so strange; I saw it with my own eyes, but I can still hardly believe it's true. You're... wolves."

"You'll get used to it." Noah shrugged. "Especially once your wolf is called. When you can shift too, it'll seem as natural as anything."

I nodded, although I was a little doubtful of that. "I guess so."

Jackson shoved the last bite of food into his mouth. "Wanna see it again?"

My heart stuttered in my chest. "What? Your wolves?"

"Yeah." He grinned mischievously, looking over my head at Noah, who stood on the other side of the bed. "What do you say? Should we show her?"

Noah ran a hand through his spiky blond hair. "I don't know, Jackson. In a hotel room?"

"Aw, what difference does it make? Sure, it's not as impressive to see a wolf in a hotel room as out in their element, but whatever. The lady hardly got a chance to see what she's in for. Let's show her."

Noah sighed. I got the impression Jackson was the instigator and troublemaker of the group, but at the moment, I was totally on his side. When he and Rhys had come back to camp the other day and shifted, I'd been in such a state of shock that I'd barely been able to take in the details of their wolf forms. And as terrifying as it was to think of being trapped in a small hotel room with two large, dangerous animals, my curiosity overrode my nerves.

"Come on, Noah." I met his gaze, biting my lip. "Please?"

Something shifted in his gray-blue eyes. His expression softened, and I knew he was going to give in because I had asked.

That thought pleased me way more than it should have. I was trying to keep up some level of barrier between myself and the four men who had barged into my life two days ago. But the walls I put up kept slipping. It was hard not to let these men take center stage in my life and my mind when they were literally the only people I knew outside of Strand.

"Yeah, okay. Close your eyes, Scrubs."

I furrowed my brow. What? Why couldn't I watch? Was this some sort of magic trick? They'd shifted yesterday in plain view.

Noah read my expression again and chuckled. "I mean, hell, you can keep your eyes open if you want. Most shifters don't give a shit about nudity, but I wasn't sure if you were quite there yet."

My cheeks flamed. *Duh. Right.* They probably had to take off their clothes to shift, and Noah was just trying to make sure I was comfortable.

I swallowed hard. Part of me wished he hadn't said anything, because now that he'd warned me, I really felt like I *should* close my eyes.

But if I was absolutely honest with myself? I didn't want to.

Because I want to watch the shift happen, my inner voice argued unconvincingly. *I just want to see how it works. That's all.*

It had absolutely nothing to do with wondering what their tanned skin and defined muscles looked like when they weren't covered up with clothes. Or wondering what their—

Oh Jesus.

Praying my face wasn't as red as it felt, I squeezed my eyes shut. I heard a chuckle that I was pretty sure came from Jackson, and then rustling sounds as the two men removed their clothes. Even though I couldn't see them, I swore the air in the room changed the second they were naked. As if it became charged with some kind of low-level electricity.

Goose bumps popped out across my skin, and my breath hitched.

Then another noise filled the space. A sort of whooshing,

cracking sound. I waited for one of them to tell me I could look, only realizing how silly that was when a cold nose bumped my hand.

Of course. They couldn't speak anymore. Not in these forms.

My eyes flew open, and I looked down at the two massive wolves. They stood on either side of the bed, and they looked so incongruous in the seedy hotel room that I almost giggled. Both of them had stark white fur, and one had his black nose pressed to my hand. His nose was cold and wet, but his breath was hot.

As I looked down, his large pink tongue swiped out to lick my hand. I let out a surprised sound that was half gasp, half laugh.

They were beautiful.

Stunning.

Incredible.

Tentatively, I scooted off the end of the bed, my gaze darting back and forth between the two massive animals. They padded toward me, meeting me as I stood up. My heart thundered in my chest, but surprisingly, I wasn't afraid. I stretched out my hand, and the wolf on my right moved closer, allowing me to stroke the soft, thick fur on his back.

I swore I felt him shiver under my touch, and he must've liked it, because he pressed closer to me. I stroked his ears, the fur as soft as silk beneath my fingertips.

A low whine sounded to my left, bringing a smile to my face.

"I haven't forgotten about you," I promised, as I turned to the other wolf—which, based on where the guys had been standing when they shifted, must be Jackson. His tongue lolled out of his mouth as his lips drew back in what was almost a smile. Leaving one hand on Noah, I scratched Jackson's wolf behind the ear as he leaned into my touch.

This was unbelievable. I felt like Snow White or something, able to commune with the wild animals of the forest.

Except these weren't *just* animals. Underneath that, they were also men.

Men I was currently fondling shamelessly. Not that either of them seemed to mind one bit.

But the surprising thing was, that realization didn't make me blush. Any discomfort or awkwardness I felt around them when they were human melted away when they were in their animal forms. And strangely, I felt more certain I could trust them now than ever. There was something so pure about them in this state. Not "pure" as in angelic—Jackson's wolf had the same wicked glint in his eyes as the man himself did—but rather, something primal. Basic. Something that existed in black and white, with none of the messy shades of gray humans were made of.

It made a pleasant shiver run up my spine, and I knelt on the floor, allowing the large wolves to press closer to me. Each beast's eyes mirrored their human features. Jackson's were dark amber and Noah's were an icy gray. Both sets of eyes watched me intently, but this time, I didn't feel like prey.

I felt strong. Powerful.

"You're beautiful," I murmured, running my fingers through the thick fur of Noah's wolf.

His large head swiveled toward mine, leaving our noses barely an inch apart. I could hear the soft *whuffs* of his breath, and the eyes that gazed into mine were bright with intelligence.

I stared into them, lost in their blue depths and uninterested in ever finding my way back.

Then his large tongue swiped out and licked my face, and the spell broke as a belly laugh erupted from my throat. I leaned back against the foot of the bed, laughing and squirming, as the wolves wagged their tails, crowding around me to lick me all over.

With no warning, the door burst open.

West stepped halfway inside, his hand still on the handle. He was breathing heavily, and at the sight of me on the floor with two of his pack mates, he stopped, his eyes widening slightly. Then he shook off whatever reaction he'd had, his gaze snapping into focus.

"We've got company. We gotta go. *Now*!"

CHAPTER THIRTEEN

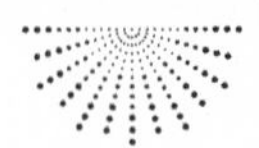

Fear soured my stomach at the urgency in his tone. He raced into the room, grabbing one of the backpacks and pulling a gun from inside it. Then he flicked the safety off and stalked back to the door, cracking it open to peer down into the parking lot.

The two white wolves prowled away from me, their hackles rising.

Swallowing my fear, I grabbed for the backpack on the bed, but West's hiss drew my attention. I looked up at him, and he shook his head.

"Leave it, Scrubs. We'll get other clothes. Get behind me. Get ready to run."

I released the strap, crawling off the bed and padding over to stand behind West. The breadth of his shoulders mostly blocked my view out the door, but I felt safer behind the muscled man than almost anywhere else.

"Three men. Armed. The blond Terminator is definitely the leader. Two are in the office, one outside."

West rattled off the information in a clipped tone. At first I thought he was talking to me, but then Jackson's wolf huffed a breath, and I realized West's report was probably for their benefit.

"Where's Rhys?" I whispered. "Did you guys steal a car?"

"Yeah."

West flashed me a look like he was surprised I was keeping my shit together. The truth was, my insides felt like ice water. But crying in a corner wouldn't get us out of here.

"The Strand hunters pulled into the parking lot right behind us, so he had to park on the far side." He jerked his chin. "He's got the engine running. We just need to get there."

"Okay." My throat was dry, and I could feel my pulse everywhere.

West narrowed his eyes at me, his dark gaze assessing. "You ever shot a gun, Scrubs?"

"N-no."

He nodded decisively, then pulled another handgun from the back of his waistband and thrust it into my hands. "*Squeeze* the trigger, don't pull it. Shoot at anyone who tries to hurt you."

The weapon felt like a brick of ice in my grip, cold and heavy. I wrapped both hands around it as the metallic taste of fear danced across my tongue. West used his gun to edge the door open a little wider, peering in the direction of the office.

"Go! Now!"

His harsh whisper almost made me jump out of my skin, but my body instinctively obeyed his command. He flung the door open, and I was hot on his heels as he raced down the raised walkway that fronted the second story rooms. The two wolves ran behind me, their padded feet almost silent on the concrete slab. Just as we were about to reach the stairs that led down to the ground floor, shots rang out.

There was a loud metallic ping as one of the bullets ricocheted off the balcony's steel railing. I screamed and ducked, raising my arms to cover my head as best I could. I still clutched the gun, and I could feel the grip sliding between my sweaty palms.

"Back! Go back!"

West screeched to a stop and pointed behind him as a man in a black shirt and fatigues rounded the stairs. The man raised his gun, but before he could shoot, West fired several rounds at him.

And then we were running again, back the way we came. This time the wolves were in front, and I could feel West close on my heels, shielding my body with his own. Heavy footsteps sounded behind us, and West wrapped an arm around me, pinning me to the side of the building with his massive frame while he raised his right arm and shot toward our pursuer.

A pained cry rose up, but before I could look to see what had happened to the man, West hauled me away from the wall, shoving me forward. I stumbled as I ran, but managed to keep my feet. The second level balcony wrapped all the way around the building, and we turned the corner at a sprint. Another set of stairs led down on this side, and I put on an extra burst of speed when I saw them.

Whoever had been behind us had been slowed—maybe stopped—by West's shots. But there were still two more men unaccounted for.

Jackson and Noah loped down the steps ahead of me. The old staircase rattled and shook as I ran after them.

But before West could join us, the big, blond, scary-as-fuck man rounded the corner on the second level, coming from the back of the hotel. He broke into a graceful, powerful run, bearing down on the wolf shifter like a runaway train. West fired at him, but the bullet went wide, barely slowing him down at all.

Shit!

As I turned around and started to run back up the stairs, something dragged me to a stop. When I glanced back over my shoulder, Noah's wolf had his jaws clamped around the back of my t-shirt.

"No! We have to help him! Let go!"

West and the Terminator were trading fire on the second level, and every loud gunshot made my stomach turn to ice. In the distance, I was vaguely aware of sirens wailing. Someone in the hotel must've called the cops.

Noah's wolfish gray eyes flashed, and if he could've spoken, I was sure he'd say something like, "Let *us* help him, you dummy."

Jackson's white form raced up the steps past me as Noah tugged me backward. I slipped down a step, my movements clumsy and awkward, before I finally relented and turned around to run on my own. An engine revved, and tires squealed as Rhys whipped the stolen car through the parking lot, driving as close to our side of the building as possible.

The wolf beside me howled, urging me on faster. I ran toward the burgundy Honda, my breath coming in short gasps. But as we neared it, a figure stepped around the side of the building.

The third man.

He wore a dark shirt and cargo pants like his compatriots, but my brain hardly registered that fact. It was too focused on the gun he held in his hand.

A wave of emotions crashed over me. Images of my mother flashed through my mind. Of the way she'd stood—her feet braced, her shoulders squared. Of the look on her face as she aimed and fired at me.

The new man raised his gun, and I brought up my own weapon at the same time, pointing it at his chest. Only a few yards separated us. At this distance, even an amateur marksman like me had a good chance of hitting their target.

But my finger resting on the trigger wouldn't move. It felt frozen, as if my hand—hell, maybe my entire body—belonged to someone else. My arm shook. All I could look at was the shiny black barrel of his gun. All I could hear was my mother's voice, rushing in my ears in a torrent of whispered promises and lies.

The man sneered, reading my expression and sensing his victory. His trigger finger twitched as he took a half-step forward.

But before his foot hit the ground, a flash of white streaked past me.

A shot rang out, and a splash of red stained the wolf's snowy fur as he leapt for the man.

The two of them went down heavily. The wolf's huge paws pinned the man's shoulders as he snarled down at our attacker. The man tried to leverage his arm up to get another clear shot, but in a flash, sharp teeth closed around his neck.

A harsh, gurgling cry split the air before cutting off abruptly. The wolf's jaws snapped together loudly as he tore out the man's throat. Blood sprayed, large droplets raining over the dirty cement. Some of it hit me, warm and wet.

I froze, staring at the man in the cargo pants and the wolf standing over him. The animal's white snout and black nose were covered in blood, the red so bright it almost looked fake.

Another shot rang out, and my body jerked. I ducked instinctively, throwing my hands over my head.

"Move!" West yelled from behind us.

He and the other white wolf tore down the stairs from the second level. They both sprinted flat out, overtaking us in a few seconds. Jackson shifted as he ran, hardly breaking stride as he transformed from a wolf back into a man. I barely had a chance to register the fact that he was naked before a hand locked onto my arm, dragging me toward the car. Noah shoved me roughly inside, diving in after me. Jackson leapt in after him and West yanked open the front passenger door, slamming his hand down on the dash.

"Go, go, go!"

Rhys was already peeling out, driving over the curb as he turned the car sharply and sped toward the main road. West leaned out the window and fired behind us, catching the blond Terminator in the shoulder as he raced across the parking lot. The man spun sideways, his momentum thrown off. He clutched at his arm and straightened, glaring after us.

"I clipped him." West pulled back inside the window, leaning back in the seat and keeping one eye on the rearview mirror. "And the other two are dead. Get us the fuck out of here, Rhys."

"On it."

Trees whipped by as Rhys rode the accelerator hard, driving us out of town.

My heart pounded so hard I swore it rattled my rib cage. I clutched the edge of the seat, turning to face the two naked men who sat in the back with me. They were both breathing hard too, their powerful, muscled chests rising and falling. Jackson had a light dusting of hair across his chest, while Noah's was smooth. Their abs contracted with each harsh breath, and a sheen of sweat covered their skin.

And Noah...

I forced my gaze up from his body to his face, and my stomach tightened. The lower half of his face was wet with blood. It dripped down his chin, splitting into small pink rivulets when it met with the sweat on his chest. The blood-covered muzzle had been disconcerting on his beautiful white wolf form, but the effect now was truly chilling.

He looked feral. Bloodthirsty.

My stare must not have been subtle, because he glanced down at me. His gray-blue eyes shuttered, the first time I'd ever seen them be anything but open and warm. West dug into one of the packs nestled on the floor by the front seat before chucking a piece of cloth back at Noah.

Noah snatched it out of the air silently and used it to wipe away the blood covering his face. A slightly pinkish tinge remained, but at least he didn't look like Hannibal Lecter anymore.

He passed the rag back up to West, exchanging the bloodied cloth for a change of clothes. West handed Jackson some clothes too, and the two men awkwardly slipped them on. I tried not to stare, but in the tiny confines of the car, there was hardly anywhere else *to* look.

"You okay, Scrubs?" Noah asked softly, lifting his ass to slide his pants up.

He was going commando, I realized. West had only given him pants and a shirt. As soon as he tucked himself away and tugged the zipper up, I was able to breathe again.

But that breath stuttered in my chest when I tried to answer him. Leftover adrenaline made me shake. I looked up into Noah's soft, sweet eyes, unable to believe that less than ten minutes ago, he'd killed a man. Murdered him in one of the most savage ways possible.

And he'd done it to save me.

I nodded shakily. "Yes. I'm sorry. I should've shot him. I tried to, but I—"

"You're not a killer." He dropped the shirt he'd been about to pull over his head, reaching over to tuck a strand of hair behind my ears. "You shouldn't be ashamed of that, Alexis. That's a good thing. We do what we have to to survive. But what this world has turned me into? I'm not always proud of it."

"Pride and survival don't always go hand in hand," Jackson added, darkness tainting his usually cheery voice.

For a moment, I let myself be stupid and give in to my impulse. I leaned into Noah's touch, letting the tips of his fingers skim my cheekbones as his large palm cradled my chin.

I shouldn't be turning to him for comfort. Not when he was also the same feral beast who'd terrified me. But my body didn't seem to understand that. It craved his strength and power, the protection he could offer in a dangerous world I wasn't equipped to survive on my own.

Reaching up, I grabbed Noah's forearm—whether to push him away or pull him closer, I wasn't sure. His eyes locked with mine, and the fingers brushing the side of my face slipped over to tangle in my hair.

He'd missed a spot with the towel. A smear of blood marred one of his cheeks, and my gaze zeroed in on it, trying to reconcile the two sides of him.

I'd seen the beauty of his wolf. And I'd seen the ugliness of it.

Both sides existed inside this sweet, kind man.

"Fuck. Strand isn't joking around."

West's voice from the front seat drew our attention, and Noah finally pulled his hand away, slipping his shirt over his head. As he did, I noticed the red line along his ribs leaking slow rivulets of blood.

Oh shit. The bullet the man had fired as Noah leapt for him. It'd just grazed his side, but another inch or two to the right and...

Panic welled up in my chest, and I forced myself not to finish that thought, focusing on the conversation going on around me.

"Strand never jokes around. They want to kill us for breaking into their fucking complex, and they want *her*"—Rhys's bright blue eyes glared at me through the rearview mirror—"back."

"That blond asshole is named Nils. I heard his buddy call him that. And he's a fucking lap dog. I'm sure of it." Jackson's lip curled.

"Did you see him shift?" Rhys asked sharply, dragging his gaze away from me.

"Nah. I bet he's under orders not to in case of witnesses. But I'd bet my last fucking dollar on it."

"What's a... a lap dog?" I asked.

Jackson shook his head in disgust. He still hadn't put his shirt on, and the muscles of his arms bunched as he pressed his fists together. "Almost every test subject in the Strand Corporation's shifter initiative was brought in against their will. Kids stolen from the foster system, homeless people swiped off the street. But there are a select few who volunteered. Who gave up their human lives to become enforcers for Strand. Ex-military, mercenary types, mostly."

"And the Terminator guy—he's one of those? He's a shifter too?"

"Yeah. Which makes him dangerous as fuck."

I shivered, picturing the huge, thick-necked man. All the guys in the car with me were big, but he towered over even them. And if he could shift too? What must his wolf look like? What would it be capable of?

"How did they know where we were? How did they find us so quickly?" I glanced out the rear window again, watching the highway disappear into the distance. I half expected to see Nils back there, gunning for us, but we'd left him behind. For the moment, at least.

"I don't know," Noah said softly. "Maybe they put out an alert for us. Maybe they're doing a broader sweep than we thought."

"The clerk could've reported us. He was eyeballing Alexis, and when I shut that shit down, he got testy."

West glanced back at me, and I remembered how he'd wrapped his arms around me possessively. Remembered the anger in the desk clerk's eyes. Would he really have called the cops out of spite?

Then I remembered the way the grungy man's lip had curled when he looked at West, and my stomach twisted. Yeah, he probably would have. And even though they hadn't come, if the Strand lap dog was monitoring police radios, he'd have heard it called in.

How could people be so awful?

I pulled my legs up to my chest, wrapping my shaking arms around my knees.

"It doesn't matter how they fucking found us. It matters that they did. And we can't let it happen again." Rhys scowled. "We need to ditch this car fast."

CHAPTER FOURTEEN

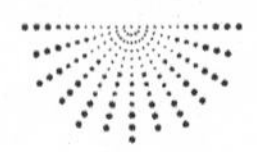

I half expected Rhys to pull over immediately after making that ominous statement. But instead, we drove for a while longer, tension filling the car as everyone kept glancing out the windows.

As Noah pointed out to me in a low voice, the one thing we had on our side was the fact that Strand likely wouldn't want to involve the police. That wasn't necessarily great news, because it meant that when they found us, they probably planned to kill us—or at least the guys. If I was truly the prized experiment they all thought I was, Strand would want me alive. But without the help of law enforcement, the corporation had fewer resources with which to hunt us.

So, definitely good news/bad news.

Noah probably thought his words would comfort me, but he must've seen my panic rising, because he trailed off into silence after that. His large hand rested gently on my knee, his fingers trailing little circles over the fabric of my pants. And that, surprisingly, did comfort me.

Despite the worry eating at my brain, my eyelids drooped, and after a while, I drifted off to sleep.

When a change in the momentum of the car woke me, my head was resting against Noah's shoulder. I blinked groggily, sitting up and trying to wipe away the little drool spot on his shirt. *Oh shit.*

His storm-gray eyes slanted down at me. Humor danced in their depths. "I've suffered worse," he whispered conspiratorially.

I grinned sheepishly, still embarrassed I'd drooled on him, but glad to see he wasn't totally grossed out by it.

"Where are we?" I queried, sitting up and stretching my cramped muscles as I peered out the windows. The scenery had changed, becoming more sparse and desert-like. The sun was low in the sky, and Rhys slowed the car as we pulled into a small roadside rest area.

"New Mexico," he said shortly.

I catalogued everything I saw, fascinated in spite of myself. I'd spent my whole life—or all the parts I could remember, anyway—locked inside the Strand complex. And now, in the space of a few days, I'd visited two states. Not that the trip had been all sunshine and roses, but still. I was getting a chance to experience more than I had in years.

We passed by a fast food place, and I had to restrain myself from pressing my face to the glass like a two-year-old. I was starving. Those donuts were the last thing I'd eaten, and that had been hours ago.

"I'll drive next," Jackson offered, as Rhys pulled into a dingy gas station.

"Be my guest."

We piled out of the car and split up. West and Noah took me to McDonalds and watched in amusement as I stared up at the menu in breathless awe. They finally ordered what seemed like one of everything on the menu, including a McFlurry for me.

As Noah paid in cash, West glanced out the large front windows.

"Here we go," he murmured.

I followed his gaze, my heart leaping into my throat. Was Nils here? Had he found us again already?

But it was just Rhys and Jackson, pulling up outside in a large gray minivan. Oh, right. The new ride we needed. I almost laughed at the sight of Jackson, with his broad shoulders, slightly crooked nose, and devilish amber eyes, sitting behind the wheel of a car more suited to a soccer-mom. But I zipped my lips shut, not wanting to draw attention from the pale-faced kid behind the counter.

We stepped outside and hustled to the van. Rhys popped the back door open for us when we approached, and we piled inside as Jackson sped off. I got the entire back seat to myself while Noah and West took the middle seats.

"Next stop, Vegas!" Jackson called out, as if he were the guide on some kind of fucked up tour.

"We've got a ways to go, so sleep more if you want." Noah handed me a bag containing several burgers and a container of fries. As if that was becoming my usual order.

Not that I minded one bit. The McFlurry was good, but so sweet and rich it made me crave something salty. And a few bites of the fries made me crave something sweet. I could see how this might become a vicious cycle.

"Aw, damn it. I wanted to see her destroy another pile of quarter pounders," Jackson complained, craning his head from where he sat in the driver's seat.

Rhys rolled his eyes. "Stop trying to watch her eat. She's not a fucking freak show."

"Hey, we're *all* freak shows," Jackson shot back good-naturedly.

I polished off my second burger quickly, listening to the guys banter back and forth. Even cranky-ass Rhys seemed to lighten up a little as they teased each other. And underneath their quick words and taunts, something else always lingered.

Love.

It was as clear as the sun in the sky to anybody who looked at them. These four men cared about each other with a bond that was almost beyond family. It was a connection born out of shared trauma and pain so deep it left permanent scars on a person's psyche.

But in the broken spaces of those scars, love had formed.

My false mother's face rose in my mind, so familiar, yet somehow alien. What had existed between us? Could any part of that be called love?

I'd thought I loved her as much as any daughter could love their mom. But now that I knew her entire presence in my life was an act, I didn't know what to make of my own feelings. And even as I was drawn into the whirlwind lives of these four men who had rescued me, I could feel myself keeping a part of my soul separate, hidden behind a wall of distrust I wasn't sure would ever crack.

How could it?

How could I ever truly trust anyone again?

But as I stretched out on the back seat of the large minivan, the men's deep voices fading into a pleasant background hum, I wanted to.

I wanted to believe I could.

~

"Hey, Scrubs. Wake up."

"Huh? What?" My eyes popped open, and I jerked awake.

Noah's face hovered over mine, and he grimaced guiltily. "Sorry. I was trying to wake you up gently."

My heart hammered in my chest. I'd been having another nightmare about the Strand complex, something I was sure would happen for a long time. I was starting to dread going to sleep, not wanting to face the horrors that waited for me in my subconscious.

"No, it's fine. You... you did."

I took his offered hand and allowed him to pull me up to a sitting position.

The car had stopped. Light streamed through the windows, and Jackson, Rhys, and West were already outside.

A yawn slipped out as I scrubbed a hand over my face. "Are we there?"

He grinned at me. "Yep."

I wasn't really sure where "there" was, except that the guys had said we needed to stop in Vegas. They had friends here who could help us somehow. How, and with what, I didn't know.

And were these the same friends who had taught them how to hot wire cars and handle firearms?

Maybe I didn't really want to meet these people.

Still, I followed Noah out of the van without protest, scrunching my brows as I swiveled my head around to take in our surroundings. We were outside what looked like an abandoned warehouse. There was nothing else around as far as I could see.

A sudden twinge of fear snaked through my stomach. Unconsciously, my gaze shot to the guys, searching for any signs of betrayal. They were all clustered around the front of the van, conferring about something in hushed voices. I'd been alone with them plenty already, but something about this location put me on edge. It was so *intentionally* remote. People only came to places like this to do things they didn't want anyone to see.

Bad things.

My hands clenched into fists, and I backed slowly away, my heart rate picking up.

West glanced up, catching sight of me. He walked toward me, sending blood rushing through my ears.

Shit. Should I run? Should I—

"Yeah, you've got the right idea, Scrubs. I'm with you." The tall black man lifted one corner of his mouth in an easy smile and draped an arm around my shoulders, pulling me farther away from the van. "Fucking idiot thinks he's gonna light the van on fire. Blow himself up, more likely. He's gonna singe all his damn hair off and be the only bald wolf shifter in the world."

He finally came to a stop and turned us around. My body was stiff as a board, and I was about to fling his arm off and make a run for it when my gaze settled on the van.

Oh.

Ohhh.

They hadn't been planning to rape and murder me, as my runaway imagination had been whispering in my mind.

They were going to destroy the van, probably to make it harder for Strand to track us.

My eyes widened.

Oh. Shit.

No wonder West had steered me far away. This was so fucking dangerous.

Jackson didn't seem the least bit concerned though. Noah and Rhys finally gave up the argument and threw up their hands, walking away from the van—although staying close enough to bail Jackson out if he needed help, I noticed.

The insane man stuck a piece of hose into the gas tank, sucking on the other end of it in a long pull before breaking away to spit out a mouthful of gasoline. He grimaced, wiping his mouth. Gas continued to flow out of the hose as he poured it liberally over the seats and floor then dragged it away from the car, leaving a messy wet trail on the ground.

"Where'd he get the hose?" I murmured.

"It was in the trunk." West's voice held a mixture of concern and amusement. "It's what gave him the stupid idea in the first place. Like we're not in enough trouble, he's always gotta be thinking of new ways to die."

"Will it actually help keep Nils from finding us?" I craned my neck to look up at West's face. My arm slipped around his waist, more naturally this time than it had back at the hotel. Maybe because this time I wasn't putting on a show.

He chuckled, his teeth bright against his dark skin. "Maybe a little. But it's more about letting off steam. We've learned by now to just let Jackson do something crazy once in a while. If he doesn't, it builds up inside him and he ends up doing something *really* stupid."

"This doesn't qualify as really stupid?" I asked, leaning closer to West as Jackson dropped the hose a few yards away from the van. Gas continued to spill from the end of it, pooling on the ground near his feet.

West's chuckle rumbled in his chest. I could feel it in my

own body, and the sensation sent warm tingles up and down my spine. Unconsciously, I gripped him a little tighter.

"Nah. For Jackson, this is pretty tame."

I looked again at the brown-haired shifter, who was currently fishing a lighter out of his pocket. It was impossible not to notice the mischievous gleam that sparkled in his eyes almost all the time—but damn, I hadn't known just how much of a thrill-seeker he was.

I kind of liked it.

But I also didn't want to see him get hurt. The thought sent a pang of fear through me that surprised me with its intensity.

Shooting a devilish grin our way, Jackson opened the lighter with a flick of his fingers, sparking a flame at the same time. He held it aloft for a second, then dropped it on the rapidly spreading puddle of gasoline.

With a whoosh, the fumes ignited. The fire spread across the surface of the gasoline like lightning, and Jackson jumped backward. The hose itself was enveloped by flames as the fire raced toward the van. It followed the line of the hose up to the gas tank, and then—

Whoosh!

The tank went up in a giant fireball, which spread quickly to the rest of the van. West and I were at a respectable distance, but all three of the others ducked as the fireball flared.

"Woohoooo!" Jackson straightened, tilting his head back

and howling. All the guys were laughing, and I realized with a start that I was too.

I felt like a kid, giddy and alive with a wild, unexplainable joy. As if destroying the car had been some sort of cleansing act, one that burned away some of the pain and betrayal of my past, leaving me with a fresh, clean slate.

The others joined Jackson as he howled, their wolves so close to the surface I could almost see them. I laughed and screamed wildly when Jackson ran toward me, pulling me from West's arms to spin me in circles.

Finally, as the huge flames engulfing the van crackled and snapped behind us, and the whoops and hollers died out. We stood watching the fire for a few moments in silence, before Rhys finally spoke.

"Great. *Now* can we go find Carl?"

CHAPTER FIFTEEN

As it turned out, Carl was the reason we were in Vegas.

The guys had done several jobs with him after they'd escaped from Strand. From the whispered information Noah shared with me in the cab ride through the city, I gathered there were some dangerously shady people the four wolf shifters had worked with over the years. Then there were people like Carl, who definitely lived outside the law but was basically a good guy.

At least, according to Noah.

The cab driver dropped us off on a dingy street lined with shops with metal grates over their windows. I crawled off Noah and Jackson's laps—there hadn't really been room for all of us in the car, but the driver didn't seem to give a shit about seat belt laws—and stepped out onto the arid, sunlit street.

I raised a hand to shade my eyes, looking up at the faded facades of the old buildings. I'd seen plenty of movies set in Vegas, but this was not at all what the city had looked like in those.

We must be a long way off the strip.

"We are," Jackson answered with a grin when I voiced my thoughts. "The glitz and glamor of Las Vegas? That's just one side of it. This"—he gestured around the street with a proud sweep of his arms—"is the real Vegas."

Huh. I wasn't sure I preferred this to the pretty, sparkling version I'd seen on TV. But then again, I'd spent my whole life being deceived by the pretty facade of an ugly place. I never wanted to be fooled like that again.

Jackson and Noah led the way toward a pawn shop with faded red lettering on the front window. I stepped after them, but my movement was arrested by a firm grip on my elbow.

Rhys pulled me toward him, his larger body dwarfing mine. Standing behind me, he lowered his head to speak low in my ear, his voice hard.

"No one you're about to meet knows shit about Strand. About shifters. About any of it. As far as they're concerned, we're just four normal guys. Don't fucking blow our cover."

I jerked my arm out of his grasp, stepping away from him. How could his touch make tingles of energy race across my skin at the same time his words made me want to throat punch him?

"Got it," I said curtly, not looking back. If he wouldn't do me the courtesy of having this conversation face-to-face, I wasn't going to either.

He didn't grab me again, but I could feel his overbearing presence behind me as we entered the shop after the others. Like he was afraid the first thing I'd do was open my mouth and start screaming about secret labs and wolf shifters.

Yeah, right. I just got *out* of the Strand complex. I had no desire to spend the rest of my life locked up in a loony bin.

A bell above the door jangled as it closed, and the occupants of the pawn shop looked up at us. Three men stood behind the counter, which seemed excessive to me, considering there were no customers in the place besides us.

Two were big. Not quite as hulking as Nils, but broad-shouldered and muscular. The third man was smaller—average height, with observant green eyes and a receding hairline that made his large forehead appear even bigger. What remained of his straight dark hair was slicked back, making him look a little like an old-school mobster. All three men were heavily tattooed.

"Hoooo-ly shit. If it isn't the four fucking horsemen!" The smaller man's brows shot up. He was probably in his late thirties, older than his two hulking buddies. "What the fuck brings you four back here? I thought you were done with this shit for good."

"What'd you always tell us, Carl?" Noah grinned, walking over to the counter and grasping the man's hand in an elaborate sort of handshake. "You never get out, you just get sidetracked. Well, we were sidetracked. Now we're back."

"Fuck yeah." Carl grinned. His pointed chin and sharp eyes gave him a slightly rodent-like appearance.

The other three men with me each said their hellos, and when Carl dropped Rhys's hand, his attention turned to me. "Well, well, well. And who's this pretty desert flower?"

Immediately, the temperature in the room chilled. My escorts had seemed happy to be here, happy to see Carl. But as if all four of them shared a single brain, each of their expressions hardened. I wasn't quite sure why. Carl wasn't leering at me the same way the hotel clerk had. His attention didn't make my skin crawl, although his perceptive eyes did seem to pick up too much.

Now his gaze darted from one of my companions to the next, assessing. Whatever he saw in their expressions made his eyebrow quirk and a slight smirk tilt his lips. Then he abandoned his question unanswered, moving smoothly to a new topic.

"What can I do for you guys? I know, I know—the first thing you wanted to do when you came back to Vegas was stop by and see your old friend Carl." He chuckled, tapping his fingers on the glass case he stood behind. "But let's get fucking real. You need something too."

The chill in the room thawed as Jackson shot him a swoony grin, batting his eyelashes. "Aw, Carl. You know us so well."

"The four horsemen? As predictable as the fucking weather." Carl smirked, jerking his head toward a door leading to the back. "Let's talk in my office."

We left the two burly men in the shop and followed Carl into a small back office. Then he shoved aside a filing cabinet that sat along a side wall and tugged open a second door. The room he led us into was much larger than the office space, and much rougher. The floor was unfinished concrete, and metal shelving units lined the walls, weighed down with a mish-mash of paper, tools, and other junk. A tall table took up the center of the space. So much crap sat on top of it I could barely see the wood beneath.

Carl sauntered in and plopped down on a stool by the table before turning in his seat to gaze at all of us. "So. What's up?"

"We need new identities, Carl." Rhys jerked his head in my direction. "And one for her too. And we need a car. Clean."

The pawn shop owner's dark brows shot up again. I had a feeling it was almost a permanent expression on him. "Damn. You guys really don't do things by fucking halves, do you? You want fries with that order?"

"Can you do it or not?" Rhys didn't even crack a smile.

I found it vaguely comforting that Rhys was as big of a dick to his supposed friends as he was to me. Maybe he didn't hate me as much as I thought.

Or maybe he just hated everybody.

But Carl didn't seem fazed by Rhys's brusque response. He stroked his chin, twisting his mouth to one side. "Yeah, I can do it. It'll cost you though. I mean, I'm not opposed to doing a favor for a friend from time to time. But that'd be five big favors, and those don't come free."

"That's fine," Noah said.

The blond-haired man stood next to me, his large body and West's bookending me. They were so close their arms brushed against mine, and even though I didn't get the impression they distrusted this Carl guy, I had the strangest feeling they were protecting me.

"Okee dokee, then. Looks like we're in business." Carl smiled. "You guys back for good, or just passing through?"

"Just passing through."

Carl's green eyes narrowed with understanding. He probably understood that "passing through" was a euphemism for "on the run." He seemed like the type who would grasp the distinction.

"Well, I can get started on this right away and have you on your merry way in a few days. Come back tomorrow and I'll take your pictures." He turned to me, cocking his head. "Any requests for a new name, sweetheart?"

"Um..." I blinked.

He laughed and shook his head, slapping his hand on a stack of papers strewn across the table as he stood. "I'm kidding! You don't really get to pick." He cast his gaze around the room, eyeing the men. "Listen, I won't ask where you picked up your mysterious fifth horseman, but I don't have to worry that anything fucked up is going on here, do I? She's all right, right?"

"She's safer with us than she would be anywhere else," Rhys said, his voice so serious that I instantly believed him.

Carl seemed convinced too, because he nodded, raising his hands placatingly. "I figured. I know you guys, but I had to ask. I may not live by the same code as every other fucking law-abiding citizen, but I do have a code. And that doesn't include abducting women."

My eyes almost bugged out of my head as I finally realized what he was getting at. He'd been making sure the guys hadn't kidnapped me.

"They didn't!" I blurted.

Well, technically, I guess they did. But it didn't feel like that at all anymore. During the chaotic race out of the Strand compound, I remembered Noah using the word "rescue." I hadn't believed it then, but that was exactly what it was.

These men were my rescuers. My saviors.

Without them, I'd still be rotting away in the house of cards I'd lived in my whole life.

I pressed closer to the two men flanking me, feeling their warm bodies answer by moving closer to mine.

Carl's keen gaze studied the three of us, taking in every detail of our interaction. "Ah. I see. Well, I'm glad to hear it, sweetheart. They really are good guys."

"I know."

A little voice in the back of my head reminded me that I'd thought the doctors at the Strand complex were good too. I'd thought my mother was good.

Don't trust them, it whispered. *Don't let them into your heart.*

But when I looked up into Noah's warm gray eyes to find him smiling down at me, I realized it might already be too late for that.

~

AFTER LEAVING Carl's pawn shop, we took another cab to a hotel off the strip.

There was a small, beat-up slot machine in the lobby, the only nod to the luxurious hotel casinos in the touristy part of Vegas. But the thing looked like it hadn't been played in years. While West and I settled into our room—which basically consisted of me sitting on one of the beds watching TV while West took inventory of the supplies and weapons in the two packs we had left—the other three went in search of food, clothes, and a few other necessities.

When they returned an hour later and dumped everything out on the other bed, I squinted at a small box curiously.

"What's that?"

"Oh, that's for you." Jackson picked it up and tossed it to me. "We didn't know what color to pick, so I hope you don't hate it."

I gaped at him. "Are you serious?"

"Very." Rhys shot me a challenging look.

Despite a strong temptation to argue, I clamped my

mouth shut. Rhys's mood had soured again after we left the pawn shop, and as annoying as his cold fronts were, this wasn't the hill I wanted to die on.

"Okay," I said simply, hopping off the bed and heading toward the bathroom with the box of hair dye clutched in my hand. "I'll be back."

It took a lot longer than I expected. I'd never dyed my hair before, and I had no idea what I was doing. Twice, Noah knocked on the door to ask if I needed help. And twice, I informed him in a slightly panicked voice that I had everything under control.

After waiting the allotted amount of time with the strange plastic cap jammed on top of my head, I hopped into the shower to rinse it all out.

A knock came as I was scrubbing my skin with the floral scented hotel body wash. I jumped about a foot in the air as the door opened a crack.

"Everything's fine! I've got it under control!" I yelped.

There was a low chuckle from the other side of the door. "Yeah, I figured, Scrubs. I just brought you a change of clothes. I'll leave 'em right here."

Noah's large hand reached through the crack, depositing a fresh set of clothes on the floor. He closed the door with a soft click, and my racing heart began to slow.

I finished up quickly, then toweled off and stepped out. When I wiped the condensation off the mirror, I hardly recognized myself. The waves of tangled wet hair falling down around my shoulders were now a pale blond, making the amber color of my eyes stand out even more against my pale complexion.

I lingered in the bathroom for a while longer, taking my time getting dressed in the jeans and t-shirt Noah had delivered. Honestly, I was a little nervous about showing the guys my new hair, for some reason. What if they hated it?

And why should it matter to me if they did?

Not wanting to think too hard about the answer to that, I forced myself to grow a pair and leave the comforting, steamy cocoon of the bathroom. The guys were spread out across the two full beds, munching on burgers and watching, of all things, a cooking show.

They looked up as I entered, and the whole room seemed to freeze. Jackson's burger hovered halfway to his mouth, which hung slightly open. Noah bit his lower lip in a way that made heat pool in my stomach. West grinned, and an expression I couldn't read passed over Rhys's face before he smoothed out his features.

I squirmed uncomfortably. "It's... I don't know, it's not really my color."

Noah hopped off the bed, his long legs carrying him toward me in a few quick strides. He reached out, catching a lock of my newly-blonde hair and rolling it between his finger and thumb. I held perfectly still, watching him, as my heart slammed inside my rib cage.

"It looks good on you, Scrubs." He tugged lightly on the strands, and a tingling feeling spread across my scalp. My breath hitched, my mouth going suddenly dry. He was standing less than a foot away from me, so close I could feel the heat coming off his body. Then he bent toward me, his voice a low whisper I knew was meant only for me. "But you'd look beautiful no matter what color your hair was."

His breath tickled my cheek as his words sent an explosion of butterflies careening around in my stomach.

I swallowed, trying to wrestle down thoughts I shouldn't be having.

Oh man. I am so totally fucked.

CHAPTER SIXTEEN

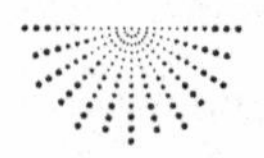

The next few days were a very strange kind of torture.

I'd never had roommates. At the Strand complex, I'd had my own private room.

Now, I was sharing a single hotel room with four men. And what was worse, except for a trip back to the pawn shop the day after we arrived so Carl could take our pictures for our new IDs, the guys had decided we needed to lay low. Which meant the five of us were boxed into the small space together. All. The. Time.

The room wasn't crazy small, but it seemed to shrink down to the size of a phone booth when we were all inside it. The men were each physically dominating, but more than that, their energy filled the space, seeming to suck up all the oxygen and making it hard for me to think straight.

To remember I needed to keep my walls up.

To remember it was a *good* thing they let me have one of the beds all to myself.

But as I lay awake at night, listening to their quiet breathing surround me like a blanket, that wasn't what I wished for at all.

I wished for Noah to crawl under the covers and wrap his arms around me. I pictured West's large body hovering over mine, his dark eyes shining down at me. I imagined Jackson's teasing chuckle in my ear as his lips brushed my hair. And Rhys?

Well, I didn't daydream about him at all. I wouldn't let myself. If there was one man out of these four I knew I shouldn't trust with my heart, it was that moody asshole. I was slowly starting to believe the others actually cared about me. That I'd gotten under their skin at least a fraction as much as they'd gotten under mine. But Rhys had made it abundantly clear on more than one occasion that he didn't want me here, didn't trust me, and didn't like me at all.

Never mind that sometimes I caught him staring at me with a look so hot I could practically feel flames licking along my skin, warming my blood all the way down to my core.

As soon as he noticed me watching him, his gaze would freeze over and his lips would harden into a line. I hated seeing that look. It crushed the part of my heart that hadn't listened to any of the warnings my brain issued—the part that had fallen for him a little bit already.

On the third night of our stay in Vegas, I lay in the darkness staring up at the ceiling like I always did, waiting for sleep to finally come. Rhys and Noah were in the other bed, and Jackson and West had made little blanket nests on the floor.

I felt anxious and unsettled. Carl hadn't given us a timeline for when he'd have everything done, and the open-endedness of our stay here was giving me flashbacks of the Strand complex. Of living in a state of perpetual waiting.

Sighing, I rolled over onto my side—and almost jumped out of my skin when I found myself staring into a set of glistening amber eyes. Jackson had sat up on the floor, and his head poked over the side of the mattress.

He chuckled at my muffled yelp and shot a look over my shoulder at the bed behind me. The two figures there were still and quiet under the blankets. Before I could register what he was doing, Jackson slipped under the covers with me, pulling them up over his shoulders.

The guys all slept in nothing but shorts—which made it impossible for me to find a safe place to look after 11 p.m. And now, I could practically feel the smooth warmth of his skin as he scooted closer, his gaze locked on my face.

"What's up, Alexis?" he whispered. "You haven't been sleeping."

I blinked, trying to figure out where to put my hands. They really wanted to press against his chest, and since I wasn't letting them do that, they twisted together restlessly.

"How do you know that?"

"I can hear your breathing. When you sleep, it evens out;

but when you're awake, it's fast. Like you're running a marathon in your head."

That was a pretty apt description, actually.

Settling for pinning my hands beneath the side of my head, I bit my bottom lip.

"Nothing's wrong," I murmured. "I'm just excited to get moving again. Not that I think things will be any better or easier once we leave Vegas, but I guess after all those years spent living at Strand, the idea of getting stuck again scares the shit out of me."

He adjusted his head on his pillow, and his long lashes caught the light of a streetlamp filtering through the curtains. "Yeah. I get that. I'd like to tell you the scars fade eventually, but I don't know if they ever do."

As he spoke, the jokester and prankster I'd gotten to know disappeared for a moment, and he seemed older. Sadder. Like he knew way too much about the worst parts of the world.

Against my will, one hand slipped out from under my cheek, pressing against the warm skin of his chest. His chest hair tickled my fingertips, and I could feel his heart thudding beneath my palm. He placed his hand over mine, trapping it before I could yank it back.

I looked away. We were already crossing way too many of the barriers I'd put in place, I couldn't let myself stare into his eyes too. "I don't expect the scars to fade. I don't even know if I want them to. If they stay forever, I won't ever forget."

He nodded, his thumb brushing against mine.

"It just makes me sad sometimes," I admitted, the honesty of my words surprising me. I was too busy trying to keep my body under control to filter my words.

"What does?" His voice was soft.

My fingers curled slightly against his chest, tears pricking my eyes. I felt raw and exposed. I had tried so hard to put up a facade of strength since these men crashed into my life—with varying degrees of success, I'd be the first to admit. But I could feel the mask slipping. As hard as I tried to roll with the punches, I was still grappling with grief and fear that sometimes threatened to wash me away in a tidal wave.

"I spent my whole life locked up. And now that I'm finally out, I don't feel like I'm really living. There are so many things I never got to do, and now, with everything that's happened... I don't know if I'll ever get to do them."

Jackson's thumb stopped moving. He grabbed my hand, and for a second, I thought he was going to bring it to his mouth and press a kiss to it. But he just held it in his, our joined hands resting on the mattress in the small space between us.

"You will, Alexis. I promise. You will."

"No." Rhys's voice was hard. "No fucking way."

"Come onnnn!" Jackson sounded almost exactly like a puppy whining to go outside and play. "Just for a couple hours!"

"I said no."

"What about you guys?" He turned to West and Noah, who were watching the exchange with amused expressions. As soon as he dragged them into it, though, their smiles dropped.

"I dunno, Jackson." Noah rubbed his neck. "We really should be laying low."

"Going to a dive bar miles off the strip *is* laying low!"

I held back a smile at that. Apparently, when Jackson had promised me last night that I wouldn't miss out on life now that I was free, he'd meant it. And now he aimed to do something about it.

"He's got a point, Rhys," West admitted grudgingly. "And besides, he's got that crazy fucking 'Jackson' look in his eyes. If we don't let off a little steam soon, he's gonna explode. Nobody needs that shit."

"Exactly!" The brown-haired shifter pointed at West in triumph.

Noah tilted his head to one side. "Yeah, that's a pretty good argument."

"Yes!" Jackson extended his other hand to point at Noah, leaping up on one of the beds to do a little dance that involved a lot of hip action and not a lot of rhythm.

I ducked my face to hide my grin. I definitely wasn't the only one going stir crazy from being cooped up like this.

Rhys shook his head, looking supremely annoyed. But then he surprised me by biting out, "Fine. One drink. Some food. That's it."

"That's all we need!" Jackson crowed, jumping off the bed and nearly bowling me over as he tackled me in a messy, enthusiastic hug. "Hear that, Alexis? We're going the fuck *out*."

Ten minutes later, we piled into a taxi. I was sure a girlier girl would've taken longer to get ready, but I had barely any clothes, no makeup, and no idea what to do with it if I'd had any. So all I did was pull my shoulder length, dyed-blonde hair into a ponytail and tug a fresh shirt out of the pile of clothes Rhys had picked up.

Why he was allowed to sneak off and go shopping, I didn't know. But since it meant I had clean underwear, I wasn't going to bitch about it.

Jackson gave the driver an address as I settled awkwardly across Rhys's and West's laps. I tried to ignore the feel of West's hand brushing the side of my leg and Rhys's breath tickling the back of my neck, and the now familiar scent of them both.

We really needed to start hailing bigger cabs.

When the driver pulled up outside a bar with half-broken neon lights in the windows and a heavy, thumping beat spilling out from inside, my pulse quickened with excitement.

I'd turned twenty-one last fall, there had been no rite of passage at a bar, no friends buying me shots. My only celebration had been a little cake my mom—no, the woman *pretending* to be my mom—and I had shared in my room. I hadn't been allowed to drink booze; not on the strict regimen

Doctor Shepherd had me on. And knowing what I knew now, the sweet memory of that day tasted bitter.

But tonight? Tonight was going to be a whole bunch of firsts.

And I couldn't fucking wait.

CHAPTER SEVENTEEN

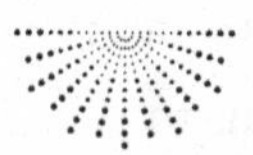

We climbed out of the car and were halfway to the bar door when a thought struck me. I slapped a hand over Noah's chest where he walked beside me, stopping him in his tracks.

"Noah! What if they card me? I don't have—"

He chuckled, prying my fingers from his shirt but keeping hold of my hand. "Don't worry, Scrubs. This isn't the kind of place that has someone checking IDs at the entrance."

Despite his reassurances, my heart hammered in my chest as we pushed through the heavy door into the bar. But no one stopped us. The place was pretty full, and the bartender barely even glanced up as we made our way toward a table in the back.

The bar was old and grungy, the dark wood floor pockmarked and scuffed. Dim light glinted off the cracked leather of the barstools, and our table wobbled badly. In one corner, a small area was cleared of tables, creating a makeshift dance floor. Music blared through speakers on the walls, so loud it was hard to hear myself think.

"I'll go order us some food and drinks!" Jackson shouted. "What do you want?"

Ugh. This is where a normal twenty-one-year-old would have any idea what to say. I had none. I could name some types of booze I'd seen referenced in various TV shows and movies, but I had no real idea what any of them were.

"Um, surprise me!" I rested a hand on his forearm and leaned up to shout near his ear.

A mischievous grin tilted the corner of his lips, and it occurred to me that I might've just made a huge mistake. Asking a guy like Jackson to surprise you was basically like asking for a huge helping of trouble. But before I could retract my request, he darted off through the crowd.

Well, shit.

I sank down into a chair at the table. Noah left to help Jackson get the drinks, and Rhys settled into another seat to glare at me. West shot me a grin, lifting his eyebrows.

It was strange. The music was too loud to carry on a regular conversation, which I would've expected to find very annoying. But there was actually something soothing about it. It took away the pressure to make awkward conversation with the man glowering at me from across the table, and my head nodded absently along with the beat.

A few minutes later, a large glass filled with blue liquid, a cherry on top, and a little pink umbrella thunked down onto the wobbly table in front of me. I gaped at it.

West rolled his eyes. "Jesus fucking christ."

"What?" Jackson shrugged innocently. "It's her first drink! Isn't it, Alexis? Her first drink should be memorable."

"It'll be memorable, all right," Rhys growled. "When she's puking it up along with everything else in her guts at three in the morning. Why didn't you get her a fucking wine spritzer or something?"

He stood up, leaning over the table to grab the neon blue drink.

But before he could take it away, I wrapped my hands around it. "No! I want it."

Truthfully, I *hadn't* wanted it until that exact moment. But I wasn't about to let Rhys tell me what I could or couldn't drink. And I wanted to prove him wrong. I could handle this. My upbringing might have stunted my social development, but I wasn't a fucking child.

I tightened my grip on the glass, lip curling up into a half snarl.

Where the hell had that come from?

Rhys saw it, and his blue eyes flashed. They were almost as bright a blue as my drink, I realized. Then I yanked my gaze away from his, capturing the straw in my mouth and taking a long pull.

I almost choked. "Sw... eet!"

Jackson grinned, looking happier than I'd ever seen him. "Yeah. It's good, huh?"

Actually, it was. The syrupy sweetness had taken me by surprise, but once I got used to it, I liked the fruity, tropical flavor. And it completely masked the taste of alcohol. I took another long swig, grinning broadly at Rhys.

"Hell fucking yeah." Jackson sat on my left side, stretching his long legs in front of him as he leaned back in the chair.

A server brought our food a few minutes later. Burgers again—not that I minded one bit. Maybe it was because we were all part wolf, but burgers seemed to be the go-to meal in this group. These were bigger and juicier than the fast food ones I'd eaten, and I took big bites in between sips of my drink.

Although I couldn't taste the alcohol in the sugary drink, I was definitely beginning to feel it.

My fingertips felt a little tingly, and my tongue seemed to be getting thicker. I had to think harder to make words, so instead of risking it, I didn't talk. I just focused on the food and drink in front of me, letting the beat of the music infiltrate my body and soul.

By the time I finished my burger, I was swaying gently along to the music. By the time I finished all the French fries, I'd picked up some of the lyrics and was singing along quietly. And by the time Jackson shoved another unclaimed burger in front of me, I picked it up eagerly, my whole body grooving to the pulsing beat.

He watched me munch and dance happily for a few

moments. Then he surprised me by plucking the half eaten burger from my hands and pulling me to my feet.

"Wha—?" I blurted.

"Come on, Lexi. If you're gonna shake it, you need to really shake it." He waggled his eyebrows at me, tugging me toward the dance floor.

Oh shit. He wanted me to dance.

With him.

In front of people.

I'd had plenty of solo dance parties in my room at Strand —which was just about exactly as pathetic as it sounded—but I'd never had reason or opportunity to dance in public.

Nerves flared in my belly, and I reached for my blue drink for a dose of liquid courage, only to find it was already empty.

Huh. I guess that must mean I already have all the courage I need.

I let that thought bolster me as Jackson led me over to the small dance floor. A few other couples were already moving together in the dimly lit space. He spun me into his arms, and to my surprise, the alcohol I'd consumed didn't make me as clumsy as I'd feared. Instead, it broke down my inhibitions, making my body feel free and loose as Jackson began to dance with me.

And that goofy dance he'd done on the hotel bed earlier?

That had been nothing.

This man could *move.*

He rolled his hips against mine, and I followed the

motion, reaching my arms up around his neck for balance. My boobs pressed up against his chest, and I could feel the muscles of his back flex and contract. My head only reached his shoulder, and his musky, masculine scent filled my nostrils, the essence of him nearly overwhelming me.

His hands found my hips, guiding me as we swayed and moved in synchronicity. The blue drink buzzed through my veins, eradicating any worries or fears.

All that was left was the music. Jackson's strong body. Bliss.

This was *definitely* another first.

We danced through one song, and then another. And with every passing minute, the fire burning underneath my skin seemed to flare a little hotter.

When Jackson twirled me away from him in a spin, I threw my head back, laughing. A grin tilted his full lips as he watched me, something wicked flashing in his dark amber eyes. But before he could pull me back into his body, another hand caught my arm.

"My turn."

West's deep voice behind me seemed to rumble like thunder, and my body liked it. A lot. I leaned back into his embrace, my eyes still locked on Jackson. The exercise had worked some of the alcohol out of my system. My head wasn't spinning, but I still felt like I was floating in a magical place where everything was beautiful and nothing bad could reach me. Where one gorgeous man held me in his arms while another watched me like he wanted to devour me.

I could live here. I never wanted to leave.

Jackson kept his gaze locked on me until West turned me in his arms, bringing all my attention back to him. One large hand splayed across my low back, pressing me close to him. His thigh worked its way between my legs, and as we swayed and moved together, little jolts zapped through my body every time my pelvis brushed against him. I clung tighter, letting the rhythm of the music and the pounding of my heart carry me away.

His fingers tangled in my hair on either side of my face as he dipped his head, bringing our faces close together. Our heavy breaths caught in the space between us, and my lips felt suddenly cold and bereft.

Kiss me! I wanted to shout.

I wanted his beautiful, full lips on me more than anything.

But if he kissed me, did that mean the others wouldn't? That was traditionally how things went, wasn't it? I wasn't too familiar with the ins and outs of dating, but when one man staked his claim, that meant other guys either backed off or fought him for it, right?

But I didn't want either of those things. I didn't want to come between these four men who had been through so much together that they were closer than family. And I didn't want the others to stop looking at me the way they did.

I didn't want to have to choose.

My tongue darted out to wet my lips, and West's eyes tracked the movement like a predator tracking its next meal.

But he didn't kiss me. Instead, he slid his hands down my curves, so low on my hips they were practically cupping my ass, and hitched me closer against his body. The move made my clit grind against his leg, and a noise somewhere between a gasp and a moan fell from my mouth, immediately swallowed up by the blaring music.

We danced like that for another song, and by the time the music changed and West drew away, I was almost panting. He smirked, like he knew exactly what he'd done to me, and backed away slowly, jerking his chin behind me.

I glanced over my shoulder to see Noah hovering at the edge of the dance floor, hands shoved into his pockets. Jackson and West were dancing solo now, but Rhys still sat at the table, his arms crossed over his chest and a stony look on his face.

Whatever. Fuck him.

Refusing to let the broody bastard pop my bubble of happy feelings, I crooked a finger at Noah, feeling more daring and reckless than I ever had in my whole life. He grinned and sauntered toward me, the lines of his body lean and strong in his blue henley and jeans.

"I guess it's true what they say." He tucked a piece of my hair back, his fingers lingering on my skin. "Blondes really do have more fun."

I laughed, grabbing his hand and wrapping it around me as we began to move to the music. "You're blond too!"

"And I'm definitely having fun."

His cheek pressed against mine as he spoke in my ear, and goose bumps raced across my skin.

Jackson was an energetic, sensual dancer. West was dominant and commanding. But dancing with Noah was different. It was like being worshipped. He moved me in time to the music, always touching me, always supporting me. In his arms, I felt safe and free at the same time.

Finally, when my skin was damp with sweat and my head fuzzy with an overload of sensations, Noah pressed a light kiss to my hair and stepped away from me. I almost fell over. I'd spent the past who-knew-how-many-minutes wrapped up in the embrace of one of these powerful men, and my body had decided it liked the feeling way too much.

Noah caught my arm with a low chuckle before steering me back over to the table. Rhys was still there, as stoic as ever. I collapsed onto a seat but popped up a moment later. Now that I was no longer caught up in a haze of music and lust, I realized I really had to pee. That blue drink had gone right through me.

"Be right back," I told the guys, then headed down a hall toward the bathrooms at the back.

The women's restroom was cramped and covered in graffiti. After emptying my bladder, I washed my hands in the too-small sink, staring at the face in the mirror. The woman with tousled blonde hair and flushed cheeks hardly looked like me.

She looked... happy.

I bit my lip, and she did the same, a grin tilting her lips.

With a giddy heart, I stepped out of the bathroom, heading down the hall back toward the bar.

As I passed the men's room, a guy stepped out. He had red hair cut in a military style and a smattering of freckles across his face. I almost collided with him, and he reached out in surprise, steadying me.

"Oops. Sorry," I muttered.

I hadn't felt tipsy while I was dancing, but I was starting to feel the effect of the blue drink again. And I didn't like it anymore. Instead of a comforting cloud of happiness, the world seemed distractingly fuzzy.

Stepping sideways, I moved to brush past the man, but he mirrored my action, blocking my way again. I looked up, forcing my eyes to focus.

"I saw you out there on the dance floor." He smiled at me, revealing slightly crooked front teeth. "Actually, I think everybody saw you. You put on quite a show."

The burgers and booze churned in my stomach as a wave of unease washed over me. Shit. I'd gotten so caught up in the moment as I danced with the guys, I'd forgotten there was a bar full of people who could see us out there.

"You like dancing?" He reached up to brush his fingers over my hair, and my heart seized in my chest. When Noah did it, the gesture was both soothing and intoxicating. But this man's touch made my skin crawl. I didn't want it.

"Yeah. It's okay." I backed away a step, breaking our contact. His hand hung in the air for a second as he watched me, a sly smile spreading across his face.

"Oh, come on. You're not going to tell me you're getting shy all of a sudden. I saw you out there."

He moved toward me, his large body crowding me down the hallway. I tried to slip past again, but his hand shot out to brace against the dingy wall, his thick arm blocking my way.

I gritted my teeth, my gaze following the line of his arm up to his neck, and finally, to his eyes. He was several inches taller than me, but I glared up at him, anger flaring inside me. I didn't like feeling trapped.

"Yeah, I do like dancing. But not with assholes like you."

The leering grin didn't leave his face. He trailed his free hand down my arm, sliding over to trace the underside of my boob. "Oh, come on, baby. You didn't even give me a chance to convince you. I bet I can change your mind."

I knocked his hand away, my heart thudding hard in my ribs with a mixture of disgust and fear. "No! I said—"

"Get. The fuck. Away from her."

CHAPTER EIGHTEEN

The voice beside us was low and dangerous, full of so much rage it made goose bumps crackle along my skin. The red-headed guy and I both whipped our heads toward the sound. Rhys stood at the end of the hallway leading into the bar, his form seeming to take up the entire space. His head was tipped down like a bull about to charge, making his eyes look slightly crazed.

"Yeah, all right, buddy." The guy boxing me in laughed. "You want to dance with her too? You'll have to wait your turn."

In three long strides, Rhys was on us. He hauled the man away from me with two fists wrapped around his shirt, slamming him into the opposite wall so hard the plaster cracked. The red-head grunted, coughing as the air was driven from his lungs. He swung for Rhys, aiming a wild haymaker at his head, but my dark protector's arm flashed up, blocking the blow.

He threw all his weight against the man, pinning him to the wall by his throat, a snarl curling his lips. "*You don't get a fucking turn*. She's ours. You don't touch her. You don't look at her. You don't speak to her."

The man's face went from red to purple, and his mouth opened and closed, seeking air he couldn't get. He thrashed back and forth, swinging wildly for Rhys's head again.

This time, his blow connected.

The punch landed on Rhys's cheekbone, snapping his head to the side. I screamed, the sound pulled from me as my own body seemed to reverberate with the force of the blow.

Rhys's hands loosened, and the guy scrambled away. Slowly, Rhys straightened. As he did, I noticed something strange about his face. At first, I thought it was just the wicked bruise blooming near his eye, but as his features caught the light, I realized that wasn't it. His face was... changing.

Oh no. Fuck, no! He was starting to shift.

A grunt fell from his lips, halfway between a growl and a moan.

"What... what the fuck is wrong with you, man?" The red-headed guy retreated a few steps down the hall, his eyes widening.

Rhys's gaze snapped to him, an animalistic rage contorting his features. He leapt forward, teeth bared.

"Rhys, no!" I grabbed onto his arm, trying to hold him back, but he shook me off.

"Oh fuck! Rhys? Shit!"

Jackson's voice sounded behind me, and the next thing I knew, all three of the guys were there, wrestling Rhys away from the other man.

"Rhys! Stay with us. Stay with us, buddy." West grabbed his face, forcing the wild shifter to meet his gaze.

But Rhys didn't seem to be in control at all anymore. His skin rippled, as if the wolf inside were trying to forcibly break out. His chest rose and fell with rapid, panting breaths, and his teeth looked like they were lengthening.

"We gotta get him out of here. Now!"

The three of them surrounded Rhys, using their combined bulk to force him down the hallway. I darted after them, panic bringing an acidic taste to my mouth. Faces turned to stare at us as they dragged him through the bar, and then we were out the door, racing toward the street.

"Cab! Get a cab!" Jackson yelled, searching the road for an oncoming vehicle.

"A cab? In his condition? Are you fucking kidding me?" West barked.

"What do you want to do, let him shift and run? You know he wouldn't go back to the fucking hotel."

"Fine. Cab."

My head was spinning, but I understood that word, at least. A yellow car drove toward us, and I raised my hand frantically.

The driver pulled over, and the guys practically shoved Rhys into the back seat. West took the front, and the rest of us piled into the back. I ended up sprawled awkwardly across Jackson and Noah's laps, all three of us focused entirely on Rhys.

His whole body trembled and shook. Droplets of sweat coursed down his face, and the large bruise by his eye morphed slightly as his body hovered on the edge of shifting. His lips were curled in a grimace, and his eyes still flickered wildly. He looked insane. Enraged. And in so much pain.

"Rhys," I whispered. "It's okay. We're almost there."

Unbidden, my hand moved up to brush the side of his face. If I'd been thinking more clearly, I probably wouldn't have done it. Rhys had made it pretty clear he hated me, and given the state he was in, I was liable to lose a couple of fingers.

But to my surprise, his body stilled under my touch. The feverish shaking stopped, and his piercing blue, wolf-like eyes met mine, locking me in their gaze. He continued to breathe raggedly through his nose, nostrils flaring, until the driver finally pulled up outside our hotel. Noah threw some cash at him before scooting out of the car. Jackson tugged me with him, and West pulled Rhys out of the back seat, supporting him as we walked quickly into the lobby of the hotel.

Halfway to the elevator, Rhys stumbled, going to his knees. My heart lurched in my chest as a low groan fell from his lips. I joined West, grabbing onto Rhys's other arm and helping to haul him up.

Our room was on the third floor, but the elevator ride seemed to take a million years. Finally, it delivered us with a ding, and we stumbled along the hallway. Noah was ahead of us, already opening the door to our room.

We burst inside, and a second later, the shift overtook Rhys.

He tore at his clothes, shredding his shirt from his body as his bones shifted and moved. His pants ripped, falling away as fur sprouted and he dropped to all fours. A keening howl burst from his lips as his mouth transformed into a snout.

"Jesus fuck." West scrubbed a hand down his face, peering out the peephole into the hallway. "Turn the goddamn TV on. A nature show or something."

Jackson dove for the remote, turning on the TV and jamming the button to turn the volume up while Rhys continued to huff and howl as he shifted.

When the change was complete, a large wolf paced restlessly in the confines of the room, padding around between the two beds and whining.

This wasn't the first time I'd seen a wolf in a hotel room. But when Jackson and Noah had shifted for me back in Texas, I'd been able to sense *them* inside their animal forms. Now? I wasn't sure Rhys was in there at all.

"What... what's happening?" I whispered.

The expression on West's face broke my heart. He looked defeated and exhausted as he watched his friend. He and Rhys were particularly close, I'd come to realize. They all were, but the two of them had a deeper bond somehow.

"It's not a perfect system," he said thickly. "We were experiments. Byproducts of trial and error. Sometimes... the wolf takes over."

"Yeah, that's what happens when people try to play god." Jackson shook his head, anger and disgust in his voice. "They fuck shit up with no idea how to fix it."

"So he might—" I swallowed. "He might not come back? He could be stuck like that?"

"Maybe." West's jaw clenched. "He's always come back before. But it doesn't help that he tried to hold off the shift. It just made his wolf more agitated."

"Is there anything we can do?"

"No. We just have to give it time."

I nodded, sinking down onto the bed closest to the door. Rhys's wolf stalked up to me, a pained whine rising from his throat. He put his head on my knee, peering up at me with hypnotic blue eyes.

Tentatively, I reached out and rested my hand on the soft fur of his head. The wolf closed his eyes, huffing a breath.

Come back, Rhys. Please, come back.

THAT NIGHT, my dreams were a confusing mishmash of images.

The woman I'd thought was my mother smiled serenely at me while skinning a dead wolf.

Doctor Shepherd held up the cure I'd waited so long for before smashing the vial against the smooth marble floor.

Hospital hallways streaked by as I was wheeled down endless corridors, pinned helplessly to a gurney by thick leather straps.

Long, vicious needles injected poison into my bones, forcing them to crack, break, and reform.

When I woke, I was clutching two handfuls of soft fur, my face buried in a fuzzy neck. I sucked in a breath as tears streamed down my cheeks, trying to keep my sobs silent.

Rhys's wolf turned to look at me, cocking his head as he took in my pale face. He blinked twice, then turned away and rested his head between his paws again.

After he'd approached me on the bed yesterday, he'd refused to let me leave his side. Every time I tried, he growled and whined, the sound so plaintive it tore my heart in two. Eventually, I'd ended up on the floor with him, the two of us nestled in a pile of blankets as we slept. The other three men had slept on the beds, although I could sense them keeping a wary eye on the two of us.

I guess I finally got my wish about getting a turn to sleep on the floor.

Too bad it was under such strained circumstances. I could practically feel the worry seeping from Noah, Jackson, and West. I knew so little about this world, and even less about being a shifter, but I didn't need to know much to understand that this was bad.

I released the handfuls of thick gray fur I was clutching, smoothing my hands over his soft pelt.

"I'm sorry, Rhys," I whispered, wishing I could go back to last night and change so many things.

Maybe if I'd dealt with the red-headed asshole myself, Rhys wouldn't have lost control like that. I'd felt small and terrified, every bit of self-confidence I'd gathered in my life extinguished in a heartbeat by a stranger putting his hands on me like I was just a thing, an object for his entertainment.

But Rhys shouldn't have been the one to challenge him. It should've been me. I shouldn't need a man—or a wolf—to rescue me.

West climbed out of bed and crouched down beside the two of us, his concerned glance taking in Rhys's wolf before flicking up to me. "You okay?"

I nodded. "What do we do now?"

"We wait." His hand fell over mine, still pressed against the wolf's side. "And you keep doing what you're doing. I'm not sure how, but you're grounding him. Keeping the last shreds of his humanity from being forced out by the wolf."

My grip tightened again, sinking into Rhys's fur. For a moment, West's fingers interlaced with mine, connecting the three of us. Then he pressed a kiss to the top of my head and stood.

"Carl should have our new IDs ready soon," he said softly. "Once they're done, we'll move out, no matter what. We can't afford to stay here any longer. Who the hell knows what that guy at the bar might've told people. We can't risk it."

The next two days passed the way the previous several had, except the boredom and tension in the cramped room had ratcheted up a million notches. I was so on edge my skin felt tight around my muscles, like I was being shrink wrapped. Rhys's wolf grew more agitated, breaking away from me every once in a while to whine and scratch at the door. He didn't like being trapped in this hotel room one bit, and I couldn't help but wonder how long it would be before the last vestiges of Rhys disappeared from inside, leaving nothing but a wild animal.

Would it turn on us then? Would it attack?

I suppressed my fear as the large gray wolf padded back over to me where I sat on the floor against the wall, nudging my face with his cold nose. He curled up beside me again, and I traced my fingers through his fur, stroking long lines down his back.

He didn't need us to be afraid of him right now. He needed us to believe in him.

Noah and Jackson went out to get food, but West wouldn't leave Rhys's side either. His dark eyes flashed with worry as he sat on the edge of one of the beds, staring at us.

We left the TV on all day, and when we all went to sleep on the second day—me on the floor again—Jackson turned the volume down a little, letting the murmur of voices and flickering blue light fill the dark room. I lay curled up next to the wolf, my head resting on his side. I could hear the deep inhales and exhales of his breath, hear him huff gently.

My eyes were just beginning to close when I felt something odd. A ripple beneath the surface of his skin, as if the bones were changing shape. My head snapped up, and I stared into the blue eyes that seemed to gleam in the darkness.

"Rhys? Please, come back."

The rippling feeling came again, and this time I saw his eyes change. For a moment, they looked almost human.

"That's it!" I whispered. "Please. I know you can do it."

His entire body shuddered, and I sat up, leaning over him. I wished there was some way I could help, but all I could do was lend my silent support as Rhys struggled with the animal that had taken over.

The shift took longer than I'd ever seen, each step toward humanity taking a massive effort. But finally, the wolf's fur receded. His limbs lengthened and shifted. His snout disappeared.

Rhys lay on the floor, his muscular body covered in a sheen of sweat. It was only after he'd finished the shift that I realized I was still hovering over him, so close my body was almost draped across his.

And he was completely naked.

For a moment that seemed to hang in the air for eternity, our gazes locked. A dark bruise shaded the right side of his face, but the blue of his irises shone bright even in the shadows.

I couldn't decipher the emotions behind his eyes, couldn't even untangle my own mixed up feelings. Relief blended with guilt, and underneath it all, there was an aching, quiet need. I wanted him to pull me into his arms—couldn't stand the breath of air that separated our bodies.

He swallowed, his hands coming to rest on my hips. A web of electricity spread out from his touch as his grip tightened, lighting up my entire body.

"Rhys!"

West's sleep-roughened voice came a second before he leapt out of bed, rushing over to us. He fell to his knees beside us, and I scrambled away from Rhys quickly. West helped him sit up, seeming completely indifferent to his nudity.

He pressed his forehead to Rhys's, gripping the back of his neck. The disturbance woke Jackson and Noah too. They climbed out of bed and crouched beside me, watching their pack mates reunite.

Noah grabbed my hand and squeezed it, and I squeezed back, hard. Tears burned the backs of my eyes at the sight of these strong men bound together by something stronger than blood.

"Thank fuck, brother," West murmured. "I thought we lost you."

CHAPTER NINETEEN

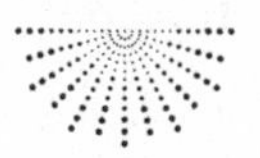

"That was Carl. IDs are ready."

Noah pressed the end call button on his burner phone—a term I only understood because I'd watched a lot of TV at the Strand.

"Good. We need to get the fuck out of here." Jackson stood, yawning and stretching.

It made the sculpted muscles of his arms and back do distracting things, and I wished like hell these guys slept in more than just shorts. It was hard to focus on anything else with them all on display like this.

After Rhys shifted back last night, the guys had insisted on giving me the bed again. Rhys had stayed on the floor, and West had joined him. I wasn't sure either of them had slept after that. I'd caught them sitting shoulder to shoulder against the wall, murmuring together in soft voices. I found myself oddly envious, though I wasn't sure exactly who or what I was jealous of. Did I wish Rhys would talk to me the way he opened up to West? Did I wish someone loved me as much as these two clearly loved each other? Maybe a little of both.

"I'll go." Rhys grabbed one of the packs from the corner of the room, rifling around inside it.

Jackson scoffed. "Uh, fuck no! Sorry, dude, but you're not going anywhere on your own for a little while. Not 'til we know you're solid."

"I'll go with him," I blurted, the words flying out of my mouth before I could stop them.

Rhys hadn't spoken to or looked at me since he shifted back. Whatever attachment his wolf had to me, the man himself definitely didn't share it, and I hated that that fact broke my heart. But as awkward as it would be, I needed to thank him for what he'd done. His attempt to stand up for me had been the thing that pushed his wolf over the edge, and I wanted him to know I was grateful. But it would be a little easier to say the words if I could get a moment alone with him.

Jackson and Noah both looked at me a little skeptically, as if they weren't sure I was the best option to protect Rhys. I couldn't argue with that, but I didn't rescind my offer.

West's dark eyes flashed to me, and I thought I saw understanding in their dark brown depths. Maybe he knew why I'd volunteered, or maybe he thought if Rhys did shift, I had the best chance of calming him down.

He nodded sharply. "That works. Just be quick. We'll get shit packed up and be ready to go as soon as you get back."

The other two nodded grudgingly. Rhys didn't say anything—apparently, he couldn't even stand to speak to me long enough to argue against me going with him.

We headed out of the hotel in silence, walking through the lobby and hailing a cab to take us to Carl's pawn shop. The ride over was quiet. I kept opening my mouth to say something and then chickening out.

When we arrived, Rhys shoved open the door and stalked toward the back of the shop, nodding curtly at the two men behind the counter as I trailed along in his wake. We found Carl in the back, perched on a stool and bent over his messy table. He hopped up when he saw us, brushing his hands off on his pants.

"Ah, Rhys! There you are! And you brought the president of your fan club again, I see." Carl smirked in my direction, and a flush warmed my cheeks. I wasn't even quite sure I knew what he meant. Were my feelings about Rhys that obvious? How could they be when I wasn't even sure how I felt myself?

"Save it, Carl," Rhys snapped. I jumped slightly, but the sharp-faced man just grinned wider. "Do you have everything?"

"Yeah, yeah." Carl dropped his teasing demeanor, getting down to business. He walked around the large table and picked up a stack of small blue booklets. "Got passports and licenses for you all. And there's a car out front. It's clean."

"Good."

Rhys tugged two large rolls of cash from his pockets,

tossing them over. Carl caught them deftly, giving them only a cursory glance before setting them on the table. Apparently, he trusted these guys enough not to count every bill before he let us leave. Honor among thieves, or however that saying went. He handed over the passports and a set of car keys, then stepped back, his gaze assessing.

"You know, kid, if you're really in trouble, maybe I can help. More than just getting you back on the run, I mean."

For a moment, Rhys's face softened. I saw a flash of hope, but it was quickly drowned out by despair. He shook his head. "Thanks, Carl. But you can't help." Then he added softly, "I'm not sure anyone can."

Carl's face fell, and he smoothed over his slicked-back hair with one hand. "Yeah, I get it. Be safe, kid, all right?" He reached out, and the two men clapped hands. Then he jerked his chin toward me. "And take care of this one. She doesn't look like she's used to our world at all. That doesn't mean she doesn't belong in it, but she'll need looking out for."

I blinked. Where had that come from? He was scarily accurate about how out of my depth I was. But how the fuck did he know that? I was beginning to feel like an open book that'd had too many pages read by strangers.

Rhys stiffened, but he squeezed Carl's hand before releasing it. "Yeah. You take care of yourself too, huh?"

Carl spread his arms, his cunning eyes playful. "When do I not?"

"Right." Rhys chuckled, slipping the IDs into his pockets.

Then he nodded once in goodbye and led me back out

through the store. Outside, he rifled quickly through the IDs before handing me a passport and license that bore my picture and the name Miranda Ney. As I tucked them into my pocket, he pressed a button on the key fob he held, making lights flash on a black truck halfway down the block. We hopped inside, and the engine roared to life.

My heart rate began to pick up as we drove back toward the hotel. This was it. My last chance to say something before we rejoined the others. My tongue felt thick in my mouth, but I finally forced my lips open.

"Thank you."

Rhys's blue gaze cut to me, but he didn't speak.

"For the other night. For sticking up for me like that. I've never had anyone do that for me before, and I want you to know that I'm grateful. I like to think I can handle myself, but I don't know what would've happened if you hadn't come down the hall at that moment. So, thank you."

I spewed out all the words I could think of in a torrent, then pressed my lips together again, my heart hammering in my chest as I waited for his response.

"Don't thank me." His voice was cool and hard. "It was a stupid mistake that could've gotten us all captured or killed. I lost control of my wolf."

My stomach twisted. "I'm sorry."

Rhys's chin dropped slightly, but he didn't look at me again. "Don't be sorry either. It's my own fucking fault." His jaw clenched. "We shouldn't have brought you with us. I knew it was a goddamn mistake. We need to stay focused and sharp, and we haven't been either."

"I didn't mean to—"

"I said it's not your fault." He sighed. "After we escaped, we spent years searching for Sariah, and when we found that complex in Austin, we spent months planning how we'd get her out. It's not your fault the whole thing went sideways in a hurry." He cleared his throat, seeming to force the next words out. "It's... not your fault she wasn't there. But now we need to regroup, start searching again, make a new plan. We don't need any distractions."

His words cut deeper than I would've imagined possible. He wasn't blaming me; he didn't even seem angry at me. But hearing him admit point-blank that he wished I wasn't here sent a sharp stab of pain through me.

"I don't know." He ran a hand through his loose black curls as he continued, seeming lost in his own thoughts. "Maybe we were wrong. Maybe you're not a shifter. Hell, you might not even be one of us."

My breath caught in my lungs. *Not a wolf shifter*? Was that possible? All the guys had seemed so sure I was when they dragged me out of the Strand complex.

Or was this just wishful thinking on Rhys's part? He was so desperate to get rid of me, maybe he was just talking himself into an excuse to leave me behind.

To get rid of me.

As much as I wanted to trust these men, as much as I'd found myself growing attached to all of them—*caring* about all of them—I'd been right to be wary. No matter how the others might feel about me, their loyalty was to their pack first. And if I wasn't even a wolf, how could I ever be part of that pack?

I ran my fingers over the edge of the passport in my hand, clinging to it like a lifeline.

At least I had this. Alexis Maddow might be utterly confused and scared out of her mind, but maybe Miranda Ney was stronger. Maybe she could find someplace to start over. To build a new life.

Alone.

CHAPTER TWENTY

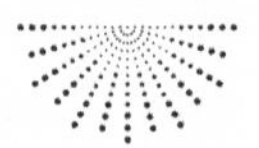

"Are we there yet?"

"Jesus fucking christ, Jackson, I will kill you if you ask that again."

"He really won't." Jackson smirked at me, his lips curling up in the devilish smile I'd come to love so much. He punched the back of Rhys's seat lightly. "He's just a big softie on the inside."

I had serious doubts about the accuracy of that statement, but I refrained from commenting. Then again, Rhys did seem to have a softer side where some people were concerned—I just wasn't one of those lucky few.

"But seriously though," Jackson added, poking his head around the side of the driver's seat and grinning innocently at Rhys. "Are we there yet?"

Keeping his right hand on the wheel, Rhys threw a punch with his left, catching Jackson on the shoulder. The amber-eyed wolf shifter yelped, pulling away to slump beside me in the back seat.

"See? What'd I tell you? A total softy."

I couldn't help but laugh. No matter how shitty my mood, Jackson could always pull some good humor out of me, even when I thought I'd lost it all.

My heart sank as I remembered that I wouldn't get to bask in his radiant smile, or in Noah's sweet presence or West's dominating protectiveness for much longer. The passport and license practically burned a hole in my back pocket, a constant reminder of the course I had set for myself.

When we'd returned to the hotel, the guys had all been waiting outside. They'd piled into the truck—I'd taken the back seat with Jackson and Noah to make the fit a little less cramped—and we'd driven out of town immediately. I could've told them then to leave me behind, but I knew not all of them would've been willing to do it. And the one thought I couldn't stand was that I might come between these men, these four bonded pack mates. They'd been through so much together, and I refused to be the thing that drove them apart.

So I wouldn't give them a choice. I wouldn't let them argue and fight amongst themselves about whether it was a mistake to bring me to the Lost Pack.

I would just leave.

My heart twinged with pain at the thought, and I nestled against Jackson's side, as if trying to soak up some comfort and strength to take with me when I went.

Oblivious to my inner turmoil, he wrapped an arm around my shoulders, tugging me closer. He leaned over to whisper in my ear, his breath warming my skin.

"Next time, you ask him."

I chuckled, but I *definitely* wasn't doing that. Rhys had made his feelings about me perfectly clear, and the last thing I wanted to do was antagonize him more.

"We just left Nevada," West shot over his shoulder from the front passenger seat. "So I'll give you a hint. No."

"Urgh!" Jackson rolled his eyes and stuck out his tongue, feigning death. Then he perked up, looking toward West. "How 'bout now?"

"This is gonna be a long fucking drive," Rhys deadpanned.

"Yeah. This is why wolves don't usually road trip." West's full lips parted on a grin, and Rhys actually cracked a smile in return.

I looked away from the sight. It made me a little sad to see, knowing he'd never smile like that at anything I said.

"So, what do you guys know about the Lost Pack?" I asked, diverting my thoughts away from things that made me want to cry.

"Not too much. Not much more than we already told you, anyway." Noah turned away from the window, shifting his gray-blue gaze to me. "We learned about it from a shifter who was held in the San Diego complex with us. I'm not sure how he heard about it, but he seemed pretty damned sure it was real."

"It makes sense. We're pack creatures by nature, and some of the early test subjects were more wolf than human." Jackson flashed a quick look toward the driver's seat, and I was sure he was remembering Rhys's lapse.

I shivered. Did they all struggle to control their animals like that, or did it affect Rhys in particular for some reason? Why him?

"Yeah. It does make sense. The only shitty part is, this guy didn't have much more than a vague idea where they were. It's not like he gave us GPS coordinates or anything." Noah grimaced. "And that was six years ago. A lot could've happened since then."

"Do you think they'll help you break back into Strand? Help you search for Sariah?"

"Who knows." Jackson's amber eyes glittered as a shaft of sunlight cut through the window. "I sure as shit hope so, though. We need to stick together. Protect our own. It's the only way to fight back."

I bit my lip. Protect their own. *Right.*

When they'd dragged me away from the Strand complex, I'd been a mess of emotions. I'd been relieved to learn I wasn't really sick, even though I still couldn't quite get used to the idea. I'd spent so much of my life seeing myself that way that it was hard to change my self-perception. I'd been living in the outside world for days now, and except for that first night, when shock and cold had overtaken me, I felt perfectly healthy.

But the flip side of that had been the discovery that I was a not-quite-human experiment—a wolf shifter.

But... was I?

Rhys had been right. They'd assumed I was a shifter because that was what most of the Strand's clandestine tests focused on. But maybe I was some other kind of experiment entirely.

I'd been horrified by the idea of being part wolf at first, but now, the idea that I might *not* be made acid churn in my gut. For the first time in my life, I'd started to feel like I belonged somewhere. And now I felt anchorless, adrift.

"—if they even care about what's going on at Strand." Noah's soft voice came from beside me, and I realized I'd gotten lost in my own thoughts while the conversation continued around me. "If they've been hiding out for years, maybe they have no interest in going back."

"Well, we won't know until we ask," West said firmly. "Anyway, maybe some of them will have information that can help us. If they've escaped from other compounds, maybe one of them knows where Sariah is. If they won't help us, we can try again ourselves. But we need to start somewhere."

"You guys never give up, do you?"

The words fell from my lips before I considered them, and I saw Rhys's shoulders tense. *Shit.*

West shot a glance at his friend before turning around to face me. "No. We don't. And we won't until we find Sariah, or... find out there's no reason to keep searching anymore."

"She's lucky." I leaned forward slightly, my words meant

for Rhys most of all. He might not like me, but I wanted him to know how much I respected his dedication to his sister. "She's lucky to have a brother like you. To have all of you on her side. I'm sure wherever she is, whatever she's going through, she knows that. She knows you're coming for her."

I reached forward and rested my hand on his arm tentatively. The muscle tensed like a rock under my touch as a small breath escaped his lips. A tear welled from the corner of his eye, and although he blinked harder, he didn't wipe it away.

THE DRIVE TOOK over eighteen hours.

We didn't stop, except for food, gas, and bathroom breaks —half of which were instigated by me. I'd never thought I had an exceptionally small bladder, but considering how shocked the guys acted every time I requested a rest stop, maybe I did.

Or they were all secretly part camel as well as being part wolf.

Jackson eventually got tired of asking if we were there yet. And when he started up again on hour seventeen, the teasing tone was gone from his voice, replaced by a restless desperation.

West had been kidding about wolves not taking road trips, but he'd had a point. Especially after nearly a week confined to a single hotel room, spending endless hours stuck in a small metal box seemed to make everyone antsy.

The guys traded off driving, although Rhys insisted on taking the longest shifts. I could feel something building inside him the closer we got to Washington—hope warring with fear.

No one asked me to drive, which was fine by me. I'd gotten a fake driver's license from Carl, but I *definitely* hadn't earned it through a demonstration of actual skill. I'd never even been behind the wheel before. And I wasn't about to start now with a truck full of people I cared about.

I dozed off in the late hours of the night, losing my struggle to keep my eyelids open. Somehow, I ended up horizontal on the bench seat in the back, my head resting on Noah's lap and my feet cradled by West's large hands. It wasn't the most comfortable position—the seat belt clip dug into my side, and the synthetic leather scent of the upholstery tickled my nose. But Noah's strong fingers tangled in my hair, massaging my scalp, and the warmth of West's palms on the skin of my ankles sent heat radiating through me, and before I knew it, I was asleep.

"Hey, Scrubs. Wake up."

The truck lurched slightly as we slowed. I jerked awake, trying to reorient myself. My sleep had been deep and dreamless, and I had no idea how long I'd been out.

Warm dawn light filled the truck. I sat up, surreptitiously checking Noah's pant leg for any drool spots. There were none, thank God. I'd already drooled on him once, and that was one more time than I wished I had.

"Are we there?" I asked, my voice rough from sleep.

"Yep! Finally!" Jackson turned back from the front passenger seat, his amber eyes lit up like the sun blazing over the horizon.

"Well, we're not actually *there*. We're at the starting point of our search. But we'll have to do the rest on foot," West corrected.

"Right." I peered out the truck window. We were in a small, mostly empty parking lot surrounded by woods. "Is this a state park?"

"Yeah. Olympic State Park. The Lost Pack is supposedly somewhere near here. We can't drive farther in, so we'll leave the truck here and start looking."

Noah smoothed back a piece of my hair that'd gotten mussed up in my sleep, then opened his door, helping me out of the large truck. While Rhys and I had been picking up the IDs, the guys had gathered supplies and packed for the journey. We had two large backpacks between us, containing food, water, and one change of clothes each, as well as some material to make a small shelter.

I couldn't help but wonder how much of this was for my benefit. If it'd just been the guys, would they have traveled even lighter? Were they making accommodations for me because I couldn't shift?

All the more reason for me to leave them to hunt for Sariah on their own. They didn't need a human tagging along after them, slowing them down.

We set off through the woods. When we were out of sight of the parking lot, Rhys and West stripped and shifted into their wolf forms. I busied myself gathering up their clothes so my gaze wouldn't stray to parts it shouldn't... although it definitely did anyway.

We walked for most of the day, following the lead of the two wolves as they kept their noses to the ground or occasionally lifted their heads to sniff the air. Unlike the first time I'd ventured through the wilderness with them, I kept pace much more easily this time. I felt better too. Stronger.

As we made our way through the forest, a silent struggle waged in my head. I'd talked myself out of sneaking away when we'd stopped at a gas station in the middle of the night. It hadn't been the right time or place, I'd told myself. But I was starting to worry that if I waited much longer, I'd never work up the courage to do what I had to.

Tonight. I'll go tonight.

It would be easier when everyone was asleep. I could slip away and get a good head start before they even noticed I was gone. And by now, they were so close to reaching their goal of finding the Lost Pack that I didn't think they'd abandon it just to come looking for me. Rhys, especially, would want to stick to their plan.

Resolve tightened my shoulders, and a silent countdown started in my head, ticking down the minutes I had left with these men who had so completely overtaken my heart and mind in the short time I'd known them. I found myself staring at each one, appreciating the masculine good looks of Noah and Jackson, and the wild beauty of Rhys and West's wolves.

By the time we stopped to make camp for the night, I was

wound up so tight I could barely move without shaking. We ate pre-packed sandwiches by the light of a small flashlight, and the food felt like lead in my stomach.

Then Noah pulled out a small down sleeping bag from one of the packs. He laid it on the ground for me before he and Jackson shifted too. It was easier for wolves to sleep in the elements than humans. None of them needed sleeping bags to get comfortable like I did.

Pushing aside my embarrassment at my weakness, I crawled inside the puffy cocoon and turned off the flashlight.

Soft huffing sounds filtered to my ears as the wolves settled in, curling up into tight circles with their noses tucked into the crooks of their back legs. I waited, trying to keep my breathing regulated. It seemed to take hours, but I didn't move until I was sure they were all asleep.

I didn't dare poke around in the dark trying to find anything to take with me. And there was nothing I needed anyway. Jackson had given me some cash at one of the rest stops so I could buy whatever food I wanted, and my IDs were still safely tucked away in my pockets. They'd given me so much already, and since I was taking the coward's way out and slipping away without saying goodbye, I wouldn't add insult to injury by stealing from them too.

Quietly as I could, I slipped my boots back on and crept away from the small, makeshift camp. When I slipped behind a large tree, I paused, turning to peer around its trunk one last time. In the darkness, all I could see were four mounds of fur on the ground—two gray and two white. If I hadn't known what to look for, I might not have even noticed them.

Four wolves. Four men. Four pieces of my heart I hadn't meant to give up.

I wished more than anything I belonged with them.

But I didn't.

CHAPTER TWENTY-ONE

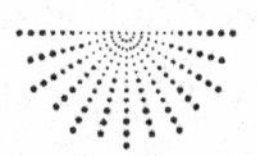

I moved slowly, stepping carefully to make sure I didn't break twigs or crunch gravel under my booted feet. As I got farther away from the camp, I picked up the pace, worrying less about making noise.

The moon was a silver arc in the sky, too small to provide much light, but my eyes adjusted eventually—enough to keep me from running into trees at least. Little ripples of fear coursed through me at the strange and unfamiliar sounds of the Washington wilderness that echoed through the darkness.

But more than that, I felt sad.

I tried not to think about the men I'd left behind, but it was an impossible goal. I missed them already.

From the moment I'd met the four shifter pack mates, they'd taken over my life completely. I hadn't had to think about where to go or what to do next because I was with them, and they had a plan. But I had liked that. At first, I'd been such a mess I needed someone else to tell me where to go and what to do—I wouldn't have been able to function without guidance. But after a while, when my shock had faded, I'd liked it for a different reason.

I'd liked being part of something bigger than myself. Being part of a group, a team... a family.

I bit my lip, my footsteps faltering as my vision blurred with tears.

You can make that for yourself, Alexis. Somehow. Somewhere.

The promise seemed empty, but I let it buoy my spirits as I wended my way through the dark forest.

Then a noise came from behind me, and I froze.

My heart sped up, hammering so hard in my chest it was hard to concentrate on anything else. I pricked my ears, searching for another hint of the sound.

There it was again.

A low, rumbling growl.

Oh shit.

I hadn't waited long enough. One of the wolves had noticed me sneak away and followed me.

Damn it. So much for leaving quietly. This was exactly what I'd hoped to avoid. I wasn't sure I'd have the strength of will to walk away if Noah turned his beautiful, sweet gray eyes on me. Or if Jackson gave me his lopsided grin.

Gritting my teeth, I turned slowly. "You caught me. I'm

sorry. I didn't want to sneak away like this, I just thought it was..."

My words fell to a whisper and died.

Yellow eyes peered out of the brush a few yards behind me.

Not wolf eyes.

These were feline. Large and predatory.

For a moment, our gazes locked—human and animal. Then, with no warning, no sign, the mountain lion leapt toward me.

I barely got my sluggish body to move in time. As the creature flew at me, teeth bared, I threw myself to the side, rolling over the rough ground. I scrambled to my feet, swiveling my head to track the mountain lion's movement as it landed gracefully. Its tail flicked, a gesture that seemed to convey annoyance. I wasn't being good, easy prey.

But that was about to change. Fuck. There was no way I could run or hide from this thing, and even less chance I could fight back. I couldn't even escape up a tree, since I was sure it was a better climber than I was.

Desperately, I searched inside myself for any sign of the wolf the guys had thought I might possess. If I was truly a shifter, now would be a really good time for me to shift—it might be the only thing that could save my life.

Please. Please, please, please!

But there was nothing there. No wolf rose up from inside my soul. Nothing changed in my body or my mind.

I was still just Alexis. A terrified woman who was about to be mauled by a wild animal.

The mountain lion leapt for me again, and I screamed, ducking behind a large tree.

But not fast enough.

Its large paw caught my arm, the force of the blow sending me reeling as its claws tore through my skin. I fell onto my butt, sharp pain flaring in my limb as my hands reached out to catch me.

Yellow eyes fixed on me, the mountain lion stalked forward. I shuffled backward, acidic fear rising in my throat.

No. I can't die like this. Not after everything I've survived so far. I may not be a wolf, but that doesn't mean I'm helpless.

Forcing down the panic threatening to overwhelm my mind, I reached out blindly, running my hands over the ground in search of some kind of weapon. The mountain lion advanced, its lips drawing back from its sharp teeth as it neared me.

My hand closed around a large dead tree limb. It was so big I could barely grasp it, but I wrapped my other hand around it too, scrambling to my feet as the mountain lion charged toward me again.

I swung the limb with all my might, connecting solidly with the animal's head.

It let out a yowl of pain, stumbling sideways as the force of my blow knocked it off balance. It regained its footing, shaking its head.

Oh fuck. Maybe I'd just made it mad.

I stood my ground, holding the heavy branch aloft with both hands even as my muscles shook with fear and adrenaline. I'd gotten lucky with that hit, and I knew it. I wouldn't be so lucky again.

The big cat yowled, an almost plaintive sound. Then it turned away from me and slunk off through the trees.

The branch fell to the ground with a thud as my grip gave out. I let out a shuddering breath, dropping to my knees on the damp, mossy earth. My sleeve was shredded and soaked with blood, but I couldn't feel any pain in my arm yet. It would set in soon enough though. I needed to get out of here.

After a few moments, I slowly staggered to my feet. My knees wobbled but held.

Then a new sound reached my ears, and my heart sank. Something else was moving through the underbrush toward me, fast from the sound of it.

I spun toward the noise just as a large gray wolf burst out of the trees. His body began to morph and ripple, and a moment later, Rhys stood before me—naked and more furious than I'd ever seen him.

He stalked toward me, bright blue eyes flashing in the dim light. "What the fuck do you think you're doing?"

When he grabbed me by the arms, I felt the pain of my injury in a rush. I hissed a cry, and he released his grip immediately, his gaze flying to my bloodstained sleeve.

"Fuck."

Without asking, he grabbed the neckline of my long-sleeved tee in both hands, ripping it cleanly down the front. I yelped, but he was already tugging the ruined shirt off me, leaving me in just my bra. The fabric chafed as he pulled it over my wounds, and I grunted in pain.

"What are you doing?" I glared at him angrily, covering my breasts with my hands.

"Bandaging your fucking injuries. What do you think?" His glare matched mine as he tore my shirt into strips.

When he was done, he pulled my arm away from my body, stepping closer to me. I was supremely conscious of his nakedness as his body crowded mine, the warmth from his skin radiating into my own exposed flesh. With practiced precision, he began wrapping the pieces of my shirt tightly around my arm. The makeshift bandages stung, but the pressure against my wounds seemed to help.

"Now, are you going to answer my question?" His sharp gaze met mine as he worked, his voice hard as steel. "What the fuck do you think you're doing?"

If one of the others had found me, I might've been tempted to deny it. But the leftover adrenaline still coursing through my veins combined with my growing anger at Rhys made me bluntly honest.

"What does it look like? I'm leaving."

He tied off one of the strips of fabric with a sharp tug that made me wince. "Like hell you are."

I slapped his hands away from my arm. I couldn't handle him touching me while we spoke. Even though his hands were rough, they set fire racing through me every time his skin brushed mine. I didn't want to feel that way, didn't want to care about him. Not when I knew how much he despised me.

"Why do you even care?" I snarled. "I'll be out of your hair forever. You got what you wanted. You got me to leave."

He froze, staring at me through the darkness. "You think I wanted you to leave?"

"Well, you made that pretty fucking obvious when you said you wished you hadn't brought me with you in the first place."

Rhys stepped closer. So close I could feel the brush of his muscular chest against mine, making my nipples go taut. So close I could feel his cock against my stomach.

Hot.

And growing hard.

He sucked in a ragged breath, dropping the pieces of my shirt and grasping my face in both hands, forcing me to look up at him.

"You're wrong, Alexis. I never wanted you to leave. I said it was a mistake to bring you with us. And it was. Because now I *never* want to fucking lose you. I want you more than I've ever wanted anyone. My wolf has practically been crawling out of my skin trying to get to you. It won't let me sleep. It won't let me focus. All I can think about is you. Your fucking fierce spirit, your beautiful goddamn eyes, your sweet as hell innocence."

I blinked. All the things he'd just said sounded like

compliments, but the tone of his voice suggested they weren't.

So why was he looking at me like he wanted to consume me?

My gaze flicked back and forth between his eyes, so close to mine I felt like I was drowning in the deep blue pools of his irises. I couldn't see anything else, couldn't feel anything else. My wound pulsed in time to my rapid heartbeat, but the pain was drowned out by the hurricane of confusion and desire tearing through me.

"I don't *want* to go," I admitted, my anger at him rising again. "You four are my only anchors in the whole world. You mean more to me than anyone. You saved my life—you *are* my life. But you're a pack. I'm not." My voice broke. "I can't stand to be alone on the outskirts of something I'm not a part of, watching and wishing I belonged. I deserve better than that."

Something feral flashed in his eyes. They shifted briefly, becoming almost wolf-like.

"You think you're not a part of us?" He grabbed my hand roughly, pressing it to his chest, where his heart pounded out a staccato rhythm. "You are, Alexis. You're a part of *this*. My heart beats for you, every fucking minute of every fucking day. You're so deep under my skin, I don't know how to get you out."

"Do you want me out?"

The words were barely a whisper, and it felt like my entire existence hinged on his answer.

Rhys stared at me, a riot of emotions churning in his ice-blue eyes.

Then he hauled me toward him, pressing my half naked body flush against his and claiming my lips in a blistering kiss.

CHAPTER TWENTY-TWO

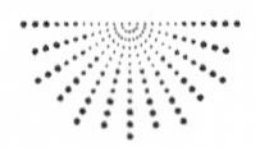

I had never been kissed before.

And in all the fantasies I'd had when I touched myself at night, locked away in my small room in the Strand compound, it had *never* been like this.

This was fire and ice, desperation and satisfaction, hate and love all wrapped into one.

Rhys's lips were warm, hungry, and demanding as he pressed them against mine, his large hands splaying across my back, keeping me upright when my knees buckled.

He licked the seam of my lips, and I opened them on a sharp gasp. He wasted no time, plunging his tongue into my mouth, deepening the kiss as he tasted me. A groan rose in his throat, and the sound strummed through me like the perfect chord, making slick wetness gather at the apex of my thighs.

I had brought that noise out of him.

I had made him lose control like this.

It was a heady thought.

And he wasn't the only one out of control. I felt drunk, high out of my mind as my tongue battled with his, sucking in breath through my nose like I was suffocating.

I was a virgin by circumstance, but as inexperienced as I was, my body responded instinctively, doing what felt good. I rolled my hips against him, seeking friction against my clit, and one of his hands slipped lower, cupping my ass and helping me work myself against his bare leg. His thick, hard cock pressed into my side, and he groaned. Stars exploded in my vision as the pressure on my clit sent fire bolts of pleasure zinging through my body.

Rhys tore his mouth away from mine, grabbing a fistful of my blonde hair and tugging it back to expose my neck for him. He trailed his lips over my jaw and throat, breathing heavily, nipping and licking the sensitive skin.

"Fuck, Lexi. Fucking Christ. You taste better than I imagined. You feel better. You're fucking perfect."

A loud voice I hardly recognized as my own cried out as he bit down hard on the junction where my shoulder met my neck. My arms were wrapped around his neck, and my fingernails dug into the smooth skin of his muscled back as my hands clenched.

He pulled away from me, leaving my throbbing clit desperate for more. But when he dipped his head to lick a warm, wet trail down my sternum and over my breast, my breath hitched. And when he unclasped my bra and tossed it aside to close his mouth around my peaked nipple, I grabbed onto his head with both hands, holding him in place as his teeth scraped across the delicate bud. His tongue lashed over it in long, full strokes, and a new kind of pleasure flowed through my nerve endings.

I had never experienced this before.

I'd brought myself to orgasm with my own hand plenty of times, but I'd never really paid much attention to my nipples. How had I neglected them for so long? *Why*? They were electric, hard as diamonds, and almost as sensitive as my clit. When Rhys brought his hand up from my ass to roll my other nipple between his fingers, my eyes flew back in my head. I was panting, unable to get enough oxygen to feed the fire burning inside me.

My hands ran through the sexy strands of black hair that tumbled around his shoulders. They brushed against my skin as he continued to suck on my breasts, alternating which one he put his mouth on.

I wriggled my hips restlessly, needing more. Needing everything.

Urged on by a primal, rising desperation, my fingers skated across the hard planes of his chest, down the ripples of his abdominal muscles, until they brushed against coarse hair and velvety skin.

Rhys released my nipple with a snarl when I closed my hand around the base of his cock. The thick organ pulsed within my grip, seeming almost to have a mind of its own. I wasn't quite sure what to do, but the feel of his cock in my hand turned me on so much I didn't want to stop. So I ran my hand lightly up to the tip, where wetness seeped from the small slit. I spread the moisture around with my thumb, using it to ease the friction as I pumped his shaft twice, tightening my grip a little.

The black-haired wolf shifter straightened, holding me close and pressing his lips to the top of my head as I worked his cock in my hand. I could feel his whole body shaking, knew how much restraint it took for him to remain still. To allow me this moment of control.

And I wasn't going to waste it.

Biting my lip, I traced my other hand down his abs, feeling the muscles contract under my touch. I let my touch travel below the base of his pulsing, veined shaft, brushing my fingers over the sac that hung there. The skin was a different texture than his cock, and when I cupped the whole thing gently in my hand, Rhys's grip on the back of my neck tightened.

Fuck. I liked this. I liked this way too much.

I grew bolder, coordinating the movements of my hands until Rhys lost control with a roar. He yanked my hands away, wrapping his arms around me and pressing me to him as he walked me backward.

My feet barely touched the ground, and the next thing I knew, the rough bark of a tree was at my back. Rhys used the leverage to pin my body even tighter against his, grinding his cock into my stomach as his lips found mine again.

This time, I didn't even hesitate, just opened my mouth and welcomed him in, letting our tongues meet in a fierce dance. I could smell something heady and musky in the air, and I wasn't sure if it was my arousal or his. Or both. But the scent spurred me on, made me ache for the one thing that promised to end this exquisite torture.

"Rhys!"

The word was a plea.

A command.

A prayer.

"Oh fuck, Lexi. I love the sound of my name on your lips. Say it again," he muttered against my mouth.

"Rhys," I groaned, rubbing my body against his, trying to find the perfect friction.

"Do you want me to take care of you? I've got you."

His voice was a rough whisper, and before I could process anything else, his hand was at the waistband of my pants, undoing the button, unzipping the fly.

Then his fingers were on my clit, and *oh holy shit*, my own hand had never, ever felt this good. Rhys's touch was rough, his fingers large and thick, and as he worked small circles over the hard nub of my clit, the pleasure was so intense it bordered on pain.

"Oh God!"

I clung to him for dear fucking life. It was the only thing I could do. Sensations ricocheted through me like fireflies trapped in a jar, and my knees shook as his fingers worked faster.

Rhys pressed his cheek to mine, his lips brushing the shell of my ear. "That's it, Lexi. Let it go. Come on my fucking hand. I want to feel you come apart."

The dirty growl in my ear, the feel of his breath ruffling my hair—it was too much. My core clenched around nothing as the most powerful orgasm of my life crashed over me, sending waves of pleasure cascading through my body. Aftershocks quaked through me, and Rhys slowed the movement of his fingers but didn't stop, helping me ride out the first orgasm into another one.

When the torrent of pleasure finally faded, I opened my eyes, which I hadn't even realized I'd squeezed shut in my ecstasy.

Rhys pulled back slightly to stare at me, a look of such raw hunger on his face that my body instantly sparked back to life. I'd just had two earth-shattering orgasms, but there was a craving deep inside me that seemed like it would never be sated.

I reached down to stroke him again, and he growled, burying his head in my neck as one large finger, already soaked with my wetness, slipped inside me.

My hand tightened around his cock. I wanted him inside me. Now.

Rhys's finger pressed deeper into my channel, and I squeezed my inner muscles around him. When the tip of his finger brushed against the barrier inside me, I felt it.

So did he.

He froze.

Then he pulled back from me, his blue eyes shadowed and his face strained with tension. "Lexi... Are you a—?"

"It doesn't matter!" I blurted, grabbing his shoulders to keep him close.

And it didn't. I was a virgin because I'd never had the chance to be anything else. I'd been focused only on getting well during my years in the Strand complex, and the opportunities for dating—or even casual hookups—had been pretty much nil in that place.

But I wasn't some precious, delicate object. I didn't need to be treated like an innocent flower.

And I wanted this. I wanted Rhys buried inside me, needed to feel that connection between us. Maybe then I'd believe all those words he'd said earlier—stop fearing that at any second he'd flip again and go back to ignoring me or shooting me angry glares.

But it was happening already. I could see the shutters falling over his beautiful blue eyes, blocking me out again, hiding his feelings.

He pulled his finger out of me, and I felt so empty I wanted to weep. I clung harder to his arms, but he brought his hands up, breaking my grip. Then he backed up several paces, leaving me slumped, half-undressed, against the large tree.

Rhys stood naked before me. The moonlight filtering through the trees cast his muscled body in sharp light and shadows. His large cock glistened in the light, wet from his precum.

He was still hard. So hard. He had to want me as much as I wanted him.

So why was he backing away?

Tears stung the backs of my eyes, the emotional rollercoaster that had started with the mountain lion's attack finally catching up with me. I didn't understand what had just happened, but I felt sick as I stared across the small clearing at the darkly beautiful man before me.

There couldn't have been more than a couple yards between us, but the space felt so vast I worried we'd never cross it again.

I gritted my teeth, forcing myself to speak without crying. "Rhys. It's okay. I want—"

But he cut me off with a sharp shake of his head. "Fuck. I shouldn't have come after you. This was a fucking mistake."

My heart cracked in half, the pieces falling into the vat of acid churning in my stomach. Goose bumps broke out over my flushed, sweaty skin, and I felt horribly exposed.

I pressed my hands over my breasts, leaning back against the tree as if I could somehow get the trunk to absorb me. When I spoke, my voice was harsh in the quiet night air.

"You're right. You shouldn't have. Next time, *don't*."

His nostrils flared, and for a moment, I thought he was going to stride across the distance and sweep me back up in his arms.

But he didn't.

He remained rooted to the spot, his gaze burning into me until he finally spoke.

"Come back to camp." His voice was low and rough. "I can't let you just wander off into the woods at night. Especially not injured. My pack mates would fucking kill me."

Right. He was worried about how they would feel. Not how I would feel.

But I *was* injured. Rhys had destroyed my shirt to bandage my wounds, and I didn't have an extra change of clothes with me. Even if I did, I'd been stupid to think I could really make a go of it on my own with nothing more than an ID and less than a hundred dollars in cash. Stupid to think I could even make it back to civilization alive.

And even if it wasn't at all in the way I wanted, Rhys had extended me an invitation to stay with him and the others. I couldn't throw that away just because my heart was a splintered, acid-soaked mess.

"Fine."

The word burned as if my throat were coated in glass.

Rhys didn't say anything else. He continued to stare at me as the muscles and bones beneath his skin rippled. Fur sprouted, and a moment later, the large gray wolf with piercing blue eyes stood in the center of the clearing. He blinked once, then turned and padded away.

Just before he disappeared into the darkness, he stopped, glancing back over his shoulder.

Waiting for me.

My hands shook as I searched through the dark underbrush for my bra. I found it tossed haphazardly over a small bush, brushed off the small twigs and leaves that'd gotten caught in the delicate fabric, and put it back on.

Then I followed the wolf through the forest, walking on leaden feet.

CHAPTER TWENTY-THREE

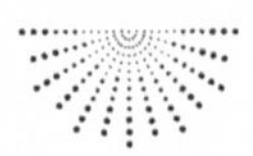

The other three were still sleeping when we got back to our makeshift camp an hour later. I grabbed my spare shirt from the pack and threw it on over the knotted, bloody fabric wrapped around my arm.

Then I slipped my boots off and crawled back into my sleeping bag, curling up into a little ball inside the tight cocoon of down-filled fabric. I pulled the top over my head, finally releasing the tears that had been held back for too long.

They tracked silently down my face in hot streaks before getting lost in the tangle of my hair, and by the time they subsided, exhaustion stepped in to take the place of grief. My eyelids fell closed, and I slipped into a dreamless sleep.

When I woke again, it was to the sound of quiet voices.

My head throbbed like it always did after a long cry, and my eyes felt puffy and swollen. The wound on my arm had settled into a dull ache, but the pain sharpened when I shifted.

"What the hell happened to her?"

"I don't know."

"She's got fucking twigs in her hair. And that's blood on her arm. She wasn't wearing that shirt last night either. So what happened?"

"I said I don't know, Jackson," West repeated, his voice a deep whisper. Concern filled his tone, making guilt twist in my stomach.

If everything had gone according to my plan, I wouldn't have been here when they woke up. I wouldn't have had to see their disappointment. Their hurt. Their worry. Now I'd have to admit that I tried to sneak off without even saying goodbye, and I honestly didn't know if they'd ever forgive me.

Slowly, I shifted in my sleeping bag. As soon as I moved, warm hands were on me, and when I opened my scratchy eyes, dark brown irises gazed down at me. West helped me sit up, his hands achingly gentle as he made sure not to brush against my injured arm.

"What happened, Scrubs? Are you okay?" He smoothed the tangled mess of hair back from my face, eyes scanning over me as he searched for other wounds.

I nodded, his tenderness piercing my heart like a knife. Jackson knelt just behind West, gnawing on his lip like he was going to take a bite out of it. New tears burned as they leaked from my eyes.

West tugged me into his arms, pulling me onto his lap

with the sleeping bag still wrapped around my lower body. He pressed my head to his chest, murmuring sweet reassurances in my ear until I finally gave a shuddering breath and pushed away from him.

"I'm..." I swallowed. "I'm okay. I got hurt last night. Out in the woods. I—"

"She heard a noise."

Rhys's deep voice cut me off, and I blinked, craning my neck to look up at him. He stood with Noah a few feet behind West and Jackson, staring at me with inscrutable eyes.

"What kind of noise?" West turned to look up at him too.

"She wasn't sure. So she woke me up and we went to investigate. A mountain lion came out of nowhere and attacked. She fought it off, but it got in a good swipe at her arm."

West's brow furrowed, and he stared hard at Rhys. But Rhys didn't take his burning gaze off me.

"Jesus fuck!" Jackson's mouth dropped open. He looked at me like he couldn't decide whether to be horrified or impressed. "You fought off a fucking mountain lion?"

I hauled my focus away from Rhys to look at Jackson. "Um, yeah. For a little bit. It was just adrenaline, really. I didn't do much."

"Not much besides fighting off a fucking mountain lion. Goddamn, Alexis. You're kind of a badass." He ruffled my hair before pulling me off West's lap and lifting my injured arm to examine it. "Hey, Noah. Grab the kit."

Noah plucked a few things from the small first aid kit in one of the packs and dropped to his knees beside me. He rolled up my sleeve, revealing the strips of fabric Rhys had tied around my arm the night before. They were stained a brownish red.

The blond man grimaced. "This is gonna hurt, Scrubs. I'm sorry."

Jackson held my hand while Noah went to work unwinding the makeshift bandages from my upper arm. He'd been right. It did hurt. The fabric felt like it'd melded with the open flesh of my wounds, and even though he peeled off each piece carefully, I had to bite my lip to keep from crying out.

When he finally had all the pieces off, he used the things he'd grabbed from the first aid kit to clean and sterilize the gashes. They were deep enough that they could probably have used stitches, but hopefully I could get away without. The skin around the claw wounds was an angry red color, the flesh bruised and traumatized. I took one look then turned my head away when my stomach dipped.

Instead, my gaze locked on Rhys's. He was still standing above us, watching me with an unreadable expression.

Why had he just lied to his pack mates? Why had he covered for me?

He must've known as well as I did how betrayed the others would feel if I admitted I'd tried to run off after everything they'd done for me.

So had he lied to protect me, or to protect them?

Or to protect himself?

I couldn't find any clue on Rhys's face, which was as blank as a statue. Only when his gaze drifted down to my injured arm did his expression shift, a look of pain passing over his face so briefly I was sure I must've imagined it.

Thankfully, the small first aid kit they'd brought included gauze and an actual roll of Ace bandages. Noah carefully wound the bandage around my arm, securing it by tucking in the end. Then he looked up at me, his sweet gray-blue eyes stormy.

"There you go. Good as new, Scrubs."

He gripped my chin, his thumb sliding up to brush lightly across my lower lip.

"I still can't believe a mountain lion went after you." Jackson shot a glance at Rhys. "Were you shifted when it attacked?"

Rhys hesitated only a fraction of a second before saying, "Yeah, I was in wolf form. But I was a little ways off, following a scent. By the time I got to her, she'd already hit it with a massive branch."

"We should stick together from here on out," West said firmly. "*All* together. Predators are a lot less likely to attack if they don't think they'll win."

"A-fucking-men to that." Jackson shook his head, still staring at me like I was his new hero.

I blushed slightly, enjoying the look on his face way too much.

If he knew the truth... The voice in my head whispered again, and my smile dropped.

"You think you can keep going?" Noah asked, bringing my attention back to him.

"Yeah." I nodded emphatically.

I wasn't going to hold them up on top of everything else. And although my arm blazed with pain from all the handling, I could already tell this new bandaging would help a lot. I'd be fine.

"Seriously badass." Jackson beamed at me before helping me out of the sleeping bag.

He stuffed it back into its little carrying sac while I laced up my boots. By the time I was done, everyone else was ready to go too.

West handed me a granola bar as we started off through the woods again. "Here. Breakfast."

"Thanks." I took it gratefully, then hesitated. "Wait, what about you guys?"

His full lips tilted up in a smile, and for a moment, I could sense the wolf within the man. "Oh, don't worry about us. We'll hunt for ours."

When I'd dreamed of a life outside the Strand complex, it had never been quite this... rugged.

We spent the next four days making our way through the wooded, mossy Washington landscape, combing the forest for the Lost Pack, and I realized I'd gone from one extreme to another—from being cooped up inside nonstop to spending every second in the vast wilderness.

As weak as it probably made me to admit it, part of me missed the easy, simple comfort of the Strand complex. A place where I'd had a roof over my head, my own room, and meals provided on a regular basis.

Out here, there were no walls in sight, but also no roof to protect me from the elements. Wind blew blonde strands of hair into my face, the sun beat down on the back of my neck, and bugs crawled over leaves and branches. The wolves I traveled with didn't seem to give these things a second thought, but to me they were foreign, exciting—and often terrifying.

West hadn't been kidding when he'd said the four of them would hunt for their food. The first time I saw Jackson's wolf dash off into the woods and return with a dead rabbit clutched in his jaws, I almost fell on my face. It was a stark reminder, as if I needed it, that these shifter men were predators themselves.

It was hard to ignore the fact that I was the weak link in our little group. They'd had to pack food and a special water bottle with a filter attached just for me, not to mention the sleeping bag and first aid supplies. And even with those considerations, I struggled to keep up. I never once complained, but by the fourth day, I could feel my energy flagging. My injured arm ached constantly, my muscles were sore, and my feet had developed blisters. My food supply was also dwindling. When it ran out, I could eat what the men hunted—but we'd have to make a fire to cook it, something I knew they'd hoped to avoid since it could call unwanted attention to us.

If they weren't holding back for me, would they have found the Lost Pack already?

The question ate at my mind, and I found myself spending the hours as we walked searching for some hint of a wolf inside me. But I couldn't find anything, and no matter how much I concentrated, wished, or begged, my body refused to shift.

Finally, I worked up the nerve to ask Noah for tips.

I'd barely spoken to Rhys at all over the past four days, and he seemed like he could hardly look at me. West and Jackson were currently in wolf form, sniffing out a path ahead of us while Rhys brought up the rear.

Noah tilted his head, his face scrunching up as he considered my question. "Tips? Huh, I don't think I have any. Sorry, Scrubs. It's not like learning to drive a car or something. It's more like learning to get along with a whole new side of yourself."

"But how can I get along with it if I can't even find it? If it doesn't even seem to be there?" I tried to keep the plaintive tone out of my voice, but I wasn't entirely successful.

Noah slipped an arm around my shoulders. "It's in there, Scrubs. I'm sure of it. It just hasn't been called yet."

"You said that before. What does that mean? Called?"

"I don't think it's an official term or anything. Fuck, I'm not sure what word those bastard doctors at Strand have for it. But it's the best way we can describe what it feels like." He looked down at me, his gray-blue eyes serious. "Think about it this way. When you were at Strand, they injected you with something that started changing your DNA. You're carrying that around with you all the time now. And someday, when the time is right, the wolf that's been lying dormant inside you will be called to the surface."

That made me feel a little better. If it was dormant, that explained why I couldn't feel it at all. Except...

"What if it's never called?"

He pulled me closer, pressing a kiss to my hair. "It will. You just gotta have faith."

It was strange. I hated what the Strand Corporation had done—*was* doing—to innocent, unwilling test subjects. I hated that I'd been lied to and held as an unwitting captive for most of my life. Maybe I should consider myself lucky if I'd somehow escaped the effects of their DNA-altering experiments.

But I still found myself wishing fervently for my wolf to show herself.

I wrapped my arm around Noah's waist under the backpack he carried, enjoying the way his muscles shifted and moved as he walked beside me. "Thanks, Noah. I—"

A wolf's howl broke through the forest ahead of us, making my heart stutter.

Noah's ears perked, and his eyes widened. "That's Jackson."

I hardly had time to be amazed that he knew the sound of his pack mates' howls. Before I could process anything, we were running through the woods toward the sound.

Rhys pulled up alongside us, and the three of us burst into a clearing where Jackson and West stood. West had his nose pressed to the ground, and Jackson broke off as he swung his lupine head toward us.

"What? *What*?"

My heart beat hard in my chest as I glanced around the clearing, searching for some sign of danger.

But Jackson's wolf padded over to nudge my hand with his nose, bushy tail wagging. He didn't seem afraid at all. In fact, he looked as excited as a puppy.

West looked up, his dark eyes meeting mine before he sniffed the ground again. Then he threw his head back and let out a full-throated howl. A second later, Jackson joined in, their voices rising through the air in perfect harmony. It called to something deep inside my soul, the sound so beautiful it made tears prick my eyes.

Movement in the woods around us caught my eye, and I peered into the underbrush.

Nearly a dozen new wolves emerged from the forest and padded toward us, surrounding us in a loose circle within the open space of the clearing. The largest one cocked its head, sharp hazel eyes taking us all in. Then it too howled. The sound was picked up by all the other wolves, their combined voices rising into the sky like a blessing and a prayer all in one.

The Lost Pack.

We had found them.

CHAPTER TWENTY-FOUR

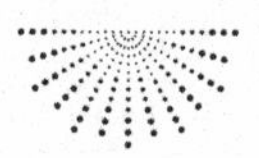

My gaze darted from my four companions to the new wolves, hope and joy filling me like helium in a balloon.

The Lost Pack does exist. We did it. We found other shifters.

I knew that's what they were, even though none of them were currently in their human forms. There was an intelligence—a *humanity*—in their eyes that no other animal on earth possessed. The mountain lion who'd attacked me the other night had been all animal, but these wolves were more than that.

The howls finally died out around us. West and Jackson's bodies shivered as they shifted, and I had to work hard not to glance at their finely shaped asses. I didn't care what any of them said, I wasn't sure I'd ever get used to the whole "shifting back naked" thing.

But this wasn't the time for ogling. We were newcomers to this pack, and although the men had seemed certain we'd be welcomed here, I wasn't ready to totally let my guard down yet.

Noah caught my eye and nodded, seeming to read my thoughts. But he looked hopeful too as he jerked his chin toward the wolf who seemed to be the leader of the newcomers, directing my attention that way. Muscles and bones rippled under reddish-brown fur until a woman stood naked before us.

The shifter woman was tall, with long auburn hair that fell down her back. She looked like she was probably in her late thirties, and a crescent shaped scar curved around the right side of her face, starting at her temple and sweeping down across her cheek.

She looked like an *actual* badass, and the hard glint in her gaze told me that trust was an emotion she'd abandoned a long time ago. But her voice wasn't unkind when she spoke.

"Welcome, wanderers. Who are you? What are you doing here?" She made no move to cover herself, keeping her gaze fixed on the five of us.

"We're escapees from the San Diego Strand complex. We heard rumors about the Lost Pack, and we came to find you. We seek asylum and aid." West dipped his head deferentially.

The woman cocked a brow. "The San Diego complex was shut down years ago. Why are you just coming to us now?"

"We spent several years living among humans, working and planning. His sister"—West gestured to Rhys—"is still captive in one of their complexes. We don't know which one. But we plan to rescue her."

The female shifter's other eyebrow rose to match the first. A look of grudging respect crossed her face, although she shook her head as she spoke.

"I doubt you'll succeed. There are too many complexes spread across the country to have much hope of finding where she is. And even if you do, you'd be foolhardy to break back into one of those places. Don't you know Strand would be all too happy to run tests on wolves who'd spent years living in the wild?"

"It doesn't matter. We're still going to try."

Rhys's voice grated roughly, and I wished I could reach out and take his hand. Wished he'd accept that kind of support from me. But I knew he wouldn't.

"So if you're planning to break into Strand, why are you here?" the woman pressed.

"Because we need help."

Several emotions crossed over her face in quick succession, but she didn't comment. Instead, she nodded her head sharply, as if deciding something.

"I'll bring you to alpha Elijah. You'll have to ask him about that. Although..." She hesitated, grimacing slightly. "I wouldn't get your hopes up."

Great.

I wasn't sure if she issued the warning because *she*

wasn't interested in helping us, or because she knew the pack alpha wouldn't be. It made sense in a way. If the Lost Pack had formed out of escaped wolf shifters, it stood to reason that they wouldn't want to go back. That they'd want to sequester themselves away, avoiding any risk of detection by Strand.

But if we all did that, the corporation would just continue on with their experiments. More innocent people like Sariah would remain locked up in complexes all over the country.

I glanced hopefully at the pack mates with me. I'd never met anyone as driven, powerful, and charismatic as them. If anyone could convince the alpha to help, it would be these men.

Jackson nodded, although I thought I detected a hint of sarcasm in his voice when he answered, "Got it. Thanks."

"I'm Val, by the way," the woman supplied.

We all introduced ourselves as she listened gravely. Then her body shivered as she shifted back to wolf form.

Jackson and West followed suit, but Rhys and Noah both remained in human form. I wondered if they were doing it to hide the fact that I couldn't shift. If everyone did, and I was the only one who didn't, it would be pretty fucking obvious there was something off. The two men had also come to stand beside me, boxing me in between them in a surprisingly protective stance.

Well, surprising from Rhys anyway.

The rest of the Lost Pack wolf shifters fell into a loose group around us as we followed Val through the woods. After about twenty minutes of walking, the scenery around us changed.

"Woah." I blinked, staring at our surroundings.

Normal wolves definitely didn't live like this.

Small shacks had been constructed out of wood and stone. They all looked extremely primitive, nothing like what people with access to the proper tools could build—but there was no mistaking what they were.

Houses. We were in a small, makeshift village.

"It's our human side," Noah murmured beside me, picking up on my thoughts. "In most of us, it's as strong as the wolf. And humans crave dwellings. They have since the early days of man."

I nodded absently, too busy gazing around at the small village as we passed through. All the buildings were well camouflaged, blending into the landscape of the forest closely enough that I was sure no one passing by in a plane overhead would notice anything amiss. Smart.

What a strange dichotomy shifters lived with—the wild balanced with the civilized.

Several inhabitants of the Lost Pack village looked up as we walked through. Some were in wolf form and some were human, but I noticed there were no children among them.

Val led us to a structure slightly larger than the others we'd passed. There was no door, just an open arch with a flap of fabric hung over it, and she stepped through it; our other wolf escorts remained outside while we followed their leader.

The interior of the structure was just as rough as the

outside. Stumps created makeshift chairs, and a roughly constructed cot lay against one wall. A man with a thick beard and wild brown hair glanced up as we entered. His gaze shifted from Val to us, and he stood quickly.

"What's this?"

Val whined, then shifted back. Jackson and West followed suit. The female wolf shifter dipped her head in obeisance to the man before pulling a simple robe from a hook by the door. Noah and Rhys dug into the backpacks they carried and handed Jackson and West clothes.

They dressed while Val spoke.

"Alpha Elijah, we found these five in the woods. They say they escaped from a Strand complex and came looking for us. They want our help."

The man scratched at his beard. He looked older than Val, maybe late forties, and he was the perfect embodiment of the word "grizzled." Actually, now that I thought about it, everyone I'd seen so far in this little village looked like they'd been through some shit.

Hell, I could relate to that.

"Where did you come from?" the alpha asked. "There hasn't been a breakout of a Strand complex in years. They got smarter once they realized how strong and resourceful their little 'experiments' were."

"We're from San Diego. We escaped in a mass breakout six years ago," West answered, tugging his shirt down over his lean abs. Then he jerked his head toward me. "She's from a complex outside Austin."

He didn't give more details than that. I could tell no one in this room completely trusted the others yet. We'd come here to ask for help, but West wasn't going to reveal our full story until he made sure we'd received a welcoming reception.

Alpha Elijah scratched at his beard with large, blunt fingers, tipping his head back to eye the five of us. "You been livin' among humans then?"

"Yeah."

"So what finally brought you to our neck of the woods? Why now?"

Val turned her head slightly, rubbing the back of her neck. She almost looked disappointed, like she sensed what was coming and didn't want to be here for this. My stomach sank. She knew her alpha better than we did, and she'd flat out told us not to get our hopes up.

"Because we want your help." Rhys stepped forward, his sky blue eyes blazing with passion and determination. His voice was low and fervent. "My sister was in that San Diego complex, but she didn't get out when we did. The breach was on the male side of the compound, and we couldn't—"

He broke off, his jaw clenching. Then he shook his head and continued.

"As far as we know, she was still in there when they closed that complex down. She was moved somewhere else. Austin, we thought; but we were wrong. She's *still* out there, though. And we want to find her and free her. Free the rest of the shifters being held in captivity, experimented on every day like fucking lab rats."

I pulled my lip between my teeth as I glanced between him and alpha Elijah. The burly, scruffy man had crossed his arms over his chest as he listened, and now he stared intently at Rhys. Val looked down at the floor, her hands clasped behind her back.

Then the alpha let out a rough sound, half grunt and half snort.

"You've come to the wrong place, son. We're a peaceful pack." He narrowed his eyes. "We hide. We *subsist*. We offer haven to those lucky enough to escape on their own. But we don't fight Strand. It's too big. I have no interest in taking on that monster, and I won't force any of my pack to join your fool's errand."

My heart sank like a rock in my chest as Rhys blinked, stunned.

Despite his resistance to coming here, I'd seen the hope building inside him as we trekked across the country, risking everything to get here. His determination to save Sariah was so strong, and I'd prayed his passion would bleed into the wolves of the Lost Pack, convincing them to join us.

But as I gazed at the weatherbeaten, tanned face of the alpha, I realized there were some things even Rhys's passion couldn't change.

This man was as solid and stoic as a rock.

And he'd given us our answer.

CHAPTER TWENTY-FIVE

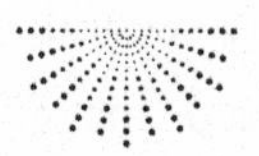

"That selfish, cowardly—"

"Keep your voice down."

"—useless fucking old man! That's it? Just, *no*? Doesn't he care about the ones left inside? Does he really think he's doing all the wolves here such a huge goddamn favor, letting them *subsist*? They deserve better than that. We all—"

"Dude! Keep your fucking voice down!" Noah interrupted again.

He glared at Rhys before brushing aside the curtain and peeking through the door of the small shack at the edge of the village. Val had led us here after our meeting with the alpha. Despite Elijah's refusal to help us, he'd told us we could stay as long as we liked as guests of the Lost Pack.

"Why? He's not my damn alpha!" Rhys looked about ready to march back into Elijah's quarters and challenge him to a fight.

"No, he's not." West's voice was calm and serious. "But he *is* the alpha to every wolf here. If you piss him off, push him over the edge, none of us are gonna make it out of here alive."

West jerked his head subtly in my direction, and Rhys's eyes shifted to me. For a second, the ice-blue of his irises softened. Then he yanked his gaze away, smoothing the rough curls of dark hair back from his face.

"Fine," he ground out, speaking at a slightly lower volume. "I'll play by his rules. I won't go starting shit." He shot a challenging look at West. "But I'm not fucking giving this up."

"Have we ever asked you to?" West shot back simply.

Rhys's shoulders slumped. He dropped his head, resting a hand on West's shoulder. West reached up to grip it tightly, and the tenderness—the solidarity—of the gesture made my heart ache.

"Rhys?"

I approached him cautiously, the way one might an escaped animal at the zoo, reaching out to grasp his arm. He stiffened at my touch, pulling his hand from West's shoulder and pacing several feet away, refusing to look at me. West's observant eyes tracked between the two of us, and a small crease formed between his eyebrows.

"What?" Rhys muttered.

I cleared my throat. There were a lot of things I wanted to say right now—top of the list being *fuck you, you moody asshole.* But I reined in my temper and quashed my heartbreak. There were more important things right now.

"I was just going to say maybe you could ask the alpha whether, if members of his pack volunteer to go, he'll let them," I said softly. "He doesn't want to force any of them to go back to Strand, and I get that—I respect that. But some of the shifters here might *want* to. Maybe some of them left loved ones behind too. Maybe they just want revenge. Maybe they don't want to have to live in fear and hiding all the time."

Jackson made an impressed face. "Hey, that's not a bad fucking idea!"

"It'll never work," Rhys bit out.

"Well, you won't fucking know until you try it, will you?" I snapped, my annoyance finally overriding my need to keep the peace. "Or I guess you could just stay in here and keep whining like a little fucking baby!"

"Oh shit!" Jackson bit his lip, his eyes bugging. He swiveled his head to look at Rhys. "Damn, dude. She fucking got your number."

Rhys froze. For a second, I wasn't sure if he was going to haul me into his arms and kiss me or throw a punch at me. But he didn't do either.

"All right." He dropped his chin in a jerky nod. "I'll go talk to Alpha Elijah."

With those words, he stalked out of the makeshift dwelling.

"Damn it, we better go with him. He's gonna lose his shit

about two seconds into that conversation if we're not there to calm him down," Noah groaned.

"Or one second," Jackson said, still grinning. He threw me a wink and a smile that made my insides warm as the two of them headed for the door.

Once they were gone, West turned to me slowly, a serious expression on his dark features. "All right. You want to tell me what's going on?"

I blinked. "What do you mean? You know more than I do."

"Not about this." He gestured around us, encompassing the shack and the Lost Pack's village around us. "What's going on between you and Rhys?"

My stomach dropped. Was the angry, heated energy between me and the dark-haired shifter that obvious? Did all of them know?

"Nothing." I shook my head and looked at the floor, letting the dyed-blonde strands of hair frame my face. "He just doesn't like me very much."

"Yeah, I'd say that's definitely *not* true." West shook his head before crossing closer to me. "Talk to me, Scrubs."

He tipped my chin up with the fingers of one hand, then ran his knuckles up my jaw to my cheek. I shivered at the strength and gentleness of his touch, and unwanted tears rose to my eyes.

"It is true, West." I looked up into his soft brown eyes, hating what I was about to say. "The night I got hurt... I didn't just hear a noise. I snuck out of camp, planning to leave. I thought it would be better that way; that I didn't belong with you four, or with the Lost Pack."

I saw his eyes widen in surprise and rushed on, knowing if I didn't get it all out at once, I never would.

"Rhys came after me. He was furious that I tried to sneak away, and he... he kissed me. He told me he can't stop thinking about me. I don't know what happened, but it was like this inferno flared up between us. It was like I couldn't get enough of him, and I thought he felt the same way. We were lost in each other, and then—"

I broke off and looked away, shame rushing over me all over again at Rhys's rejection.

"Then what?" West asked softly.

"He found out I was a virgin, and everything changed. He backed away—could barely look at me." My head lifted, my gaze almost challenging. "It's not like there's something wrong with me! I know about sex. I *want* it. I just never had the fucking chance! I'm not broken! I'm not—"

More tears streaked down my cheeks, and West gathered me up in his arms, pressing me against his strong, warm body. "Of course there's nothing wrong with you, Scrubs. You're perfect."

"Rhys doesn't think so." My voice was muffled by his shirt and his hard pecs.

"Yes, he does." West's large hand palmed the back of my head. "Believe me on that. I've seen how he looks at you." He sighed, his chest shifting under my cheek. "Rhys has been through a lot. He has a hard time... processing emotions. Especially positive ones."

"Tell me about it," I muttered, and he chuckled.

"The reason he backed off, and why he's been acting like such a dick around you since, is probably because he feels like a fucking asshole for almost taking your virginity in the middle of the woods like that."

"But I wanted him to!" I blurted, and then blushed. That had been an overshare. Especially since I was talking to Rhys's best friend... and a guy I had fantasized about more than once.

West cupped my face in his hands, tilting his head to look down at me. "It doesn't matter. It still would've been a dick move. You're too precious for that."

I scowled. "I'm not, though! I'm not a fucking delicate flower. I may have been sheltered most of my life, but I'm not that breakable."

Something shifted in West's eyes. The chocolate brown pools seemed to darken even more as his pupils dilated. His hands moved around to the back of my head, sliding through my hair.

"I didn't say you were any of those things, Scrubs. I said you were precious. And I won't take that back."

My breath hitched.

His voice was deep and low, the timbre seeming to reverberate through my whole body, lighting up my nerve endings. My core clenched, and I realized that somewhere over the course of this conversation, we'd shifted from *friend and confidant* to *man and woman.*

What had happened with Rhys the other night was still burned into my mind, branded on my body. But it didn't stop me from wishing that West would lower his face the few inches that separated us and press his perfect lips to mine.

"West..."

My voice was breathless, hopeful, lustful.

And it was the only invitation he needed.

Tightening his grip on the roots of my hair, he leaned down and kissed me.

The second man to kiss me in all my life.

It was so different than Rhys, but so perfect. West's lips were full and warm, smooth and commanding. He kissed me like we had all the time in the world, and he'd be goddamned if he rushed something so sweet.

My hands flew up to cling to his biceps, which bunched under my fingertips as he adjusted the angle of my head to take the kiss deeper.

Having learned from my experience with Rhys, I opened my mouth right away, welcoming West's skillful tongue like a long lost friend.

Jesus fucking Christ.

This was what I'd been missing all those years I was locked away in the complex for years, and in this moment, I hated everyone at Strand for that more than any of the other lies and deceptions they'd fed me.

They had kept me from experiencing moments like this.

They'd kept me from living.

But dear sweet Lord, I was living now.

I pressed my body against West's, relishing the rough, deep noises that rumbled from his chest. I wanted to see what other sounds I could pull from him. I wanted to make him feel as good as I felt.

One of his large hands slipped from my hair, trailing over my collarbone and tracing the line of my breast. I shuddered, grabbing his palm and pressing it hard against me, determined to make him believe I wasn't fragile. I could handle this. All of it.

All of them.

The thought lit an inferno inside me. I wanted them all. I hadn't even admitted that to myself until this moment, but I'd felt it building inside me for weeks. The whole time we'd been on the run together—through the horrible attack at the hotel in Texas, through weeks cooped up in too-small spaces together, through dancing and drinking and all the little moments in between—I'd been falling in love with these four wild shifter men.

And right now, one of them was kissing me like he might be falling for me too.

"West."

I breathed his name again, as though if I said it enough times, I could own it. Imprint it on my soul.

"Goddamn it, Alexis. I've wanted to do this since the day I met you."

His voice was ragged, his breathing uneven. He pulled

back for a second to stare into my eyes, and the spark in his told me he liked what he saw there.

He moved to kiss me again, but before he could, there was a commotion outside.

Raised voices moved closer.

Angry voices.

Both our heads whipped toward the door just as Rhys, Jackson, and Noah burst inside the shack, followed by alpha Elijah, Val, and several other shifters I didn't know. West's pack mates all stopped short at the sight of the two of us clearly locked in an embrace.

But then alpha Elijah stepped forward, his eyes flashing.

"She's from an *elite complex*? And you didn't check her for a damned tracker?"

CHAPTER TWENTY-SIX

Fear swept over me like a cold wind.

I had no idea what the alpha shifter was talking about, but his voice was full of both anger and fear. And the word "tracker" couldn't be good.

A sudden image from one of the countless nature documentaries I'd watched while locked up in the Strand complex flitted through my mind. A wolf being tagged with a microchip then released back into the wild so the scientists could study its movements.

Goddamn it. I wasn't an animal.

But had I been tagged like one?

"What the hell is going on?" West's arm tightened protectively around me.

The alpha's chest heaved as his gaze scanned me up and down like I was a ticking time bomb that might explode any minute.

"You all escaped from San Diego *six years ago*," Elijah boomed. "Back before Strand realized they needed to do more to keep their little pet projects from escaping. But your friends just told me *this one*"—he turned to me, his lip curling back in anger—"was stolen from an elite, underground facility. That means she's important to them, which means she's being fucking tracked!"

He strode toward me with an intentional stride, but before he reached me, all four of the men were in front of me.

"Back. The. Fuck. Off." Noah's voice was soft and dangerous.

"Not until she's dealt with. She's a threat to everyone in my pack!"

"She's not being fucking tracked!" Jackson shouted. "We've been on the run together for weeks. We were camped out in Vegas for days. If they had a tracker on her, they would've found us already."

"Unless they were hanging back," Val said softly. "Waiting to see where you'd go."

Her quiet voice cut through the angry yells, and she stepped forward, slipping between Noah and Rhys to approach me. Her hazel eyes met mine as she slid her arm around my shoulder, running her hand over the space between my shoulder blades. Her fingers pressed and massaged the skin, searching for something.

I saw the truth in her eyes before she said the words.

"She's tagged. I can feel the chip."

The ground seemed to pitch beneath my feet. Horror and fear made my skin prickle.

What? No... Please, God, no.

On top of everything, on top of all the ways the doctors at Strand had betrayed me, had broken my trust, had treated me as less than human—this was too much.

"No. No! Get it out!" My voice rose to a panicked screech as I clawed at my back, trying in vain to reach the spot where Val's fingers had pressed. "Help me! Please! *Get it the fuck out!*"

"It's too late," Elijah said, resignation and pity mixing with the anger in his eyes as he watched me.

"Maybe not." Val turned to look at him. "If we extract it now, we can have someone carry it several miles from here and destroy it. Maybe it will be enough to avoid detection."

I could barely hear her. I thrashed, arms wrapped around myself like I was in a straightjacket, fingernails scratching like knives, straining to reach the object lodged in my body.

The alpha growled in frustration before giving a decisive nod, and Val sprang into action. She turned back to me, grabbing my face in her hands.

"Okay. *Okay*! Alexis, we're going to help you. But you have to stay still, all right?"

I nodded desperately, allowing Jackson to pull my hands away from my back. My heart slammed against my ribs, as if it too were trying to force the tracker—the *parasite*—out.

"Knife." Val held out her hand, and one of the other pack members darted forward, pulling what looked like a hunting knife from a small sheath he wore. My breath picked up at the sight of it, until I was almost hyperventilating.

"Keep her calm," Val ordered, her tone clipped. "And turn her around."

Strong hands fell on my shoulders, spinning me away from her. My four wolf shifters crowded around me, steadying me, their faces filling my vision.

"It's all right, Scrubs. It'll be out soon." Noah palmed the back of my head and brought my forehead to his chest, pressing me to him.

I stared down at our feet, sucking in air and blinking tears from my eyes as Jackson and West each grabbed one of my hands. I lost track of Rhys for a second, then realized he'd gone behind me to help Val.

His hands lifted the back of my shirt, so much more gently than they had in the woods four nights ago.

"We've got you, Alexis," he whispered softly, his voice low in my ear. "We've got you, baby."

His words were a balm to my soul, and for a moment, I was able to take a full breath again.

Then Val's knife pierced the flesh of my back, tearing a ragged cry from my lips. Warm blood spilled in a stream down my back as she used the tip of the blade to root around for the tracking chip the doctors had inserted under my skin. I gritted my teeth against the pain, pressing my forehead hard into Noah's chest. My hands squeezed Jackson's and West's so hard my muscles shook.

"Shit," Val muttered. "Slippery little fucker."

I winced as the blade cut deeper. Val's fingers dug inside the incision she'd made, trying to leverage the chip out.

"Almost done." Rhys's hand gripped my wadded up shirt at the nape of my neck, his other hand bracing my shoulder as he watched Val work.

The blood trailing down my back tickled my skin, which was coated with a light sheen of sweat.

Get it out. Get it out! Get it out!

Val's fingers gouged deeper into the wound, and my knees shook as bile rose up in my throat. Finally, she let out a triumphant sound.

"Got it!"

There was a sharp, tearing feeling, and then her hands pulled away. I slumped forward into Noah's arms, weak with relief and pain.

"Shit." Val's voice turned hard. "Yeah, that's a Strand tracker all right."

"Should we destroy it now?" Noah spoke over my head, his arms wrapped around me, carefully avoiding the cut on my back. Rhys pressed a piece of cloth to my back, soaking up the blood that still leaked from my wound.

"No," the female shifter said. "If the signal cuts off now, the last known location will be right here. We need to take it at least a few miles away before we destroy it. That may not be enough, but it's the best option we have."

"I'll do it."

Four voices spoke in unison, and my heart swelled at their response. The tracker was like a blinking beacon calling "come get me" to the Strand hunters, and anyone near it would be in danger. It made painfully sweet emotions burn in my chest to know these shifter men wanted to protect me like that.

But I couldn't let them.

The tracker had been implanted in me. I was the one who'd carried it all this time, putting the men at risk. And I'd unwittingly brought it into the middle of the Lost Pack, potentially revealing their location to Strand.

"No. I'll do it." I forced myself to push away from the comforting strength of Noah's embrace. "It was inside me. I'll destroy it."

"No!" West's eyes blazed. "No fucking way. You're injured—twice over." He gestured to my bandaged arm. "You're not in any shape to go running off through the woods."

"Yeah, sorry, Alexis. None of us are gonna get on board with that." Jackson flashed me a smirk, but his eyes were anxious.

Rhys peeled back the cloth he'd been holding to my back to stem the blood flow. I hissed a breath, pulling away from his touch and turning around. A small trickle of blood still worked its way down my back, and I felt a little lightheaded. But I squared my jaw as I looked at Val.

"Give it to me."

Her hazel eyes narrowed in assessment as she handed over the small tracker chip. It was covered in blood—so was her hand—and my stomach churned as she slipped it into my palm. The thing was small and innocuous-looking. A tiny piece of metal maybe an inch long and a quarter inch wide.

I closed my fist around the blood-stained chip. "How do I destroy it?"

"Bash the fuck out of it with a rock. Don't stop until it's unrecognizable."

A savage satisfaction filled me. *With fucking pleasure.*

I strode toward the doorway, but Rhys grabbed my uninjured arm, hauling me back. His eyes were wild as he closed his hand over the fist containing the tracker. "No, Lexi!"

For a moment, I lost myself in the swirling, bright blue of his irises. This was the first time he'd looked at me since our encounter in the woods. The first time I'd seen something on his face like the expression he'd worn when he confessed how much he needed me.

"I have to, Rhys," I whispered, trying to make him understand. "Because I can't lose you either."

His entire face changed. Something lit up in his eyes that I'd never seen before, not even the night he kissed me. His hand squeezed tighter around mine, and he opened his mouth to speak when a long howl sounded outside the shack.

Two more wolf voices joined in, sending up a haunting, sustained sound like a siren.

Alpha Elijah cocked an ear, a frown darkening his roughened features. His nostrils flared.

"It's too late. They're already here."

CHAPTER TWENTY-SEVEN

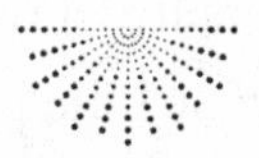

The howls outside the shack grew louder, the pitch rising as the threat neared.

Alpha Elijah roared, the sound completely inhuman. Before I could even think, he was shifting. He didn't bother stripping off first, and his clothes tore away as his body rippled and bent, fur sprouting from his back.

His wolf was enormous, with shaggy brown fur and massive paws. He raced out of the shack as one of the howling wolves cut off abruptly with a pained yelp.

Val turned to us, her face hard. "Run. As far and as fast as you can. Alpha Elijah will scatter the pack. Our rendezvous point is in Montana."

She rattled off a set of GPS coordinates, and I tried to burn them into my memory, forcing my overloaded brain to focus.

Then she raced out the door after her alpha, shifting as she ran. The other Lost Pack wolves followed.

Rhys blinked at me. His fist released mine, and I uncurled my fingers and tipped the tracker out of my palm. It fell to the rough dirt floor of the shack, its blood-soaked surface picking up dust and debris. It looked so plain and ordinary; how could that one little piece of metal have caused so much trouble?

Growls and yips came from outside, followed by an unmistakeable popping sound.

Fuck.

I'd know that sound anywhere. I heard it most nights in my dreams these days.

Gunfire.

The noise seemed to shock all of us back into action. Rhys dropped my hand as West and Noah shouldered the packs. Jackson pressed himself to the wall by the door, peering out through the curtain.

"Damn it, there are a lot of them." His voice was tense. "Armed. The blond Terminator is here too."

Nils. He seemed to be the one leading this hunt. Had it been his decision to let us get away after the hotel? To track and follow us instead?

Cold rage filled me, and I wanted to race out of our shelter and confront him, to finish what West had started back at the hotel.

To end him.

But I didn't have any weapons. I couldn't even shift.

Made in the USA
Monee, IL
10 October 2020

Running again was the only choice we had if we wanted to live.

"Here! Rhys, Noah. Help me!"

West gestured them over to the back of the makeshift wooden shack, and the three men started prying planks away from the wall, creating a hole.

The sounds of wolves and humans clashing spread out around us as the Lost Pack shifters scattered into the woods.

"Shit! They're raiding all the buildings. We gotta fucking move!" Jackson's voice was a harsh whisper, and he ducked away from the front wall, being sure to stay out of direct line of the doorway. He grabbed my hand, tugging me with him as we joined the others.

The hole in the back wall was barely big enough to squeeze through. My heart felt like it was trying to crawl up my throat as I forced myself through the small opening. The guys, with their wider frames, barely made it through. Noah and West had to remove the backpacks and pass them ahead separately. In the woods around us, whimpers and growls sounded, interspersed with human voices as the Strand's hunters called out to each other.

Shit.

Because the little village was so spread out, there wasn't exactly one central area for Nils and his men to level their attack. That meant they were probably spread out in the trees all around us. A net that would be almost impossible to slip through.

West tucked the plank of the wall back into place behind

us, and we all crouched behind the small shack. Noah scanned the woods, his gray eyes darting around quickly. When there was a moment of silence, he nodded.

"Let's go. Stick together. Stay down."

Rhys and West flanked us, guns drawn, as we ran through the forest.

I was practically folded in half, trying to make my body as small as possible. Branches scratched my face as I ran, and the back of my shirt was soaked with blood.

A shout went up behind us. Then a quick *pop pop pop*. A large hole appeared in a tree trunk next to me, splinters of wood flying as a bullet pierced the bark. I screamed, holding my hands over my head and running faster. Rhys and West fired back, the sounds so loud this close up that they made my ears ring.

"Fuck! It's Nils!" Jackson peeked over his shoulder then cursed soundly.

More gunshots burst through the middle of our group, scattering us like antelope.

A bullet grazed my leg. The sharp, stinging pain almost broke my stride, but momentum kept carrying me forward. I glanced around me but couldn't see any of the men out of my periphery. We'd been forced apart by the spray of bullets.

I couldn't stop. I couldn't think. I could only run, faster and faster, lungs burning and side cramping, breath coming in painful gasps.

Waiting.

Waiting for the bullet that wouldn't miss next time.

But no bullet came. The sound of gunshots faded, the howls around me died out. And still, I ran.

Finally, when my lungs felt like I'd inhaled fire and the stitch in my side was so acute every footfall felt like plunging a knife into my belly, I collapsed to the ground, crawling behind a fallen tree trunk to shield myself. Blood and sweat bathed my body in a thin sheen, and my hands shook as I rose up on my arms to peer over the large tree trunk.

Damn it.

There was no sign of the guys.

No sign of anyone.

Worry nearly overwhelmed me. In all the shots fired, had any of them been hit?

I should've stopped, should've—fuck, I don't know.

There wasn't anything I could've done, I knew that logically. If we'd stopped running, we'd probably all be dead. But at this moment, that almost seemed like a better option.

To die together rather than be forced apart.

I forced myself to take a deep breath, though my lungs still burned. *It's okay, Alexis. It's okay. You know where the rendezvous location is, and so do they. You'll find each other again.*

And they *would* find me. I was more certain of that than I'd ever been of anything in my life.

But I still couldn't bring myself to move farther away from the place I'd last seen them. Instead, I clung to the dead bark of the fallen tree, staring through the forest as if I could somehow call the four shifters to me by wishing hard enough.

Should I go back? Was it worth the risk?

I hauled myself to my feet, but before I could make a decision about which way to move, a twig snapped behind me.

Someone grabbed me roughly, yanking me back, and I was slammed up against a hard, muscled body. The impact made the wound in between my shoulder blades scream with pain, and I struggled against the thick arms binding my arms and chest like a vise.

"Let go!" I rasped. "Let me go!"

The Strand hunter growled, his grip tightening even more. He hauled me backward, lifting me up so my feet barely even brushed against the ground.

I was helpless. Immobilized.

A sudden memory of the red-headed asshole who'd cornered me in the bar flooded my mind. I hadn't done anything to stop him then. I hadn't fought back hard enough. But I'd promised myself I would never let that happen again.

Trying to regulate my breathing, I let my body go limp, giving up the struggle.

"That's better," the man grunted.

He loosened his hold slightly to adjust his grip on me, and in that second, I moved. I dipped my head and bit down on the flesh of his arm as hard as I could.

Blood flooded my mouth, and the man screamed. He dropped me, tearing my teeth away from the ragged wounds I'd created. Then he charged, bowling me over backward and

landing hard on top of me. His blunt face was red, and his eyes flashed with anger.

"You fucking bitch," he snarled.

I threw an elbow at his face, putting so much weight behind it that when his head whipped to the side, we both rolled over. I scrambled to my feet, but he lunged after me, grabbing me by the ankle. The breath rushed out of my body as I slammed against the damp earth of the forest floor. I coughed and scrabbled for a handhold, kicking desperately as he hauled me back toward him.

The burly hunter flipped me over onto my back, hands gripping my ankles to stop me from kicking as he loomed over me. A sneer twisted his features, and he tugged me closer.

"Now, that was not very ladylike," he chastised, his voice rough. A trickle of blood worked its way down the side of his face, and his arm was smeared with it.

He bent down to pick me up again, and I didn't even think. My hand formed a tight fist, and I rose up quickly, aiming a punch right at his crotch. I connected with dick, balls, and pelvis, and it hurt like a bitch.

But it hurt him worse.

He let out a squawk like a dying turkey and collapsed in a ball, face turning almost purple as he gasped for air and clutched at his junk. I hauled myself to my feet, my entire body quivering with exhaustion and adrenaline.

"That ladylike enough for you?" I panted breathlessly.

He didn't answer. And I didn't wait around for a reply.

I took off through the forest in a staggering run, wiping

the blood away from my mouth with my sleeve as I went. I didn't know how long what I'd done would disable the man, and I knew I didn't have it in me to kill him in cold blood, even if it would keep him from coming after me. So I needed to get away as quick as I could.

My heaving breaths and rushing blood drowned out almost every other sound. Until a new noise filtered through to my ears.

A distant cry.

"*Scruuuuubs!*"

It came from a distance, but the word was unmistakeable. Tears of relief, joy, and worry stung my eyes as I stopped, whirling around. My men. My shifters.

Damn it, they shouldn't be yelling like that. Not with the woods full of Strand hunters.

But they were alive. They were coming for me.

The call came again, so far off I could barely hear it, and I changed course, moving as quickly as I could in their direction. Hope made my heart clench in my chest. I just needed to get to them. Once we were together, we could figure out our next step.

But we *needed* to be together. And I needed to get to them before they called all the Strand hunters down on us.

My body was exhausted, and the wounds in my shoulder and back hurt like hell. I pushed that all away though, focusing on drawing in deep, even breaths as I jogged unsteadily through the woods.

But just as my stride began to even out, a figure stepped out from behind a tree ahead of me.

My heart clutched in my chest, and my feet skidded over the rough ground as I froze in place.

He was almost fifteen yards ahead of me, but the black gun in his hand was pointed directly at my chest.

"There you are. I saw what you did to Simon," Nils called, his deep voice cold and callous. "I'd blame you, but it was really his mistake. Do you know how they take down an animal in the wild, girl?" He squared his shoulders, tilting his head back slightly. "They don't get too close."

Keeping his weapon trained on me, he reached behind him, pulling what looked like a second gun from the waistband of his cargo fatigues. He brought it up beside the first, his unblinking eyes locked on me.

Then he fired.

The sound was different than any other gun I'd heard before—more of a hiss than a pop—but before I could register that fact, something sharp slammed into my shoulder. A red-feathered dart had buried itself deep within the muscle, and even as I looked down to gape at it in horror, my vision wavered as if the world around me was nothing more than a mirage.

I tried to move, to run, but when I lifted my foot, it couldn't seem to find the ground again. I stumbled and pitched sideways, the earth reappearing suddenly as it rushed up to meet me.

Dragging myself on my forearms, I crawled across the mossy forest floor until even that became too difficult.

With the last of my strength, I rolled over onto my back. Numbness spread through my limbs and infected my brain, a quiet nothingness that robbed my soul of fear, robbed my spirit of fight.

Nothing mattered.

Not the blue sky peeking through the blurry leaves overhead.

Not the sound of heavy footsteps approaching.

Not the hard, weathered face framed by blond hair peering down at me.

It was all just a dream.

Somebody else's nightmare.

My vision darkened around the edges, the blackness pulling me under as Nils's hard features cracked into a smile and he spoke again.

"*That's* how you take down a wild animal."

~

THANK YOU FOR READING!

Alexis and her harem's story crept into my brain one night and just wouldn't let me go. I absolutely loved writing this book, and I hope you loved reading it just as much! If you did, please leave a review (even a sentence or two makes a huge difference!).

And don't worry, I won't leave you hanging! Book two, *Wolf Called*, is coming soon.

In the meantime, you can dive into my complete reverse harem urban fantasy series, *Magic Awakened*, starting with the free prequel novella, *Kissed by Shadows*.

Join my mailing list, and I'll send you your FREE copy of *Kissed by Shadows*!

Want access to exclusive teasers, cover reveals, giveaways, and more? Join my reader group, Sadie Moss's Rebel Readers!

ABOUT THE AUTHOR

Sadie Moss is obsessed with books, craft beer, and the supernatural. She has often been accused of living in a world of her own imagination, so she decided to put those worlds into books.

When Sadie isn't working on her next novel, she loves spending time with her adorable puppy, binge-watching comedies on Hulu, and hanging out with her family.

She loves to hear from her readers, so feel free to say hello at sadiemoss.author@gmail.com.

And if you want to keep up with her latest news and happenings, you can join her Facebook group, or follow her on Twitter, Goodreads, and Amazon.